PLAY HOUSE

PLAY HOUSE
Saikat Majumdar

The Permanent Press
Sag Harbor, NY 11963

Copyright © 2017 by Saikat Majumdar

All rights reserved. No part of this publication, or parts thereof, may be reproduced in any form, except for the inclusion of brief quotes in a review, without the written permission of the publisher.

For information, address:
The Permanent Press
4170 Noyac Road
Sag Harbor, NY 11963
www.thepermanentpress.com

Library of Congress Cataloging-in-Publication Data

Majumdar, Saikat, author.
Title: Play house / Saikat Majumdar.
Other titles: Playhouse
First U.S. edition.
Sag Harbor, NY : The Permanent Press, [2017]
ISBN 978-1-57962-497-2
    1. Women in the theater—Fiction. 2. Dysfunctional families—Fiction. 3. Mothers and sons—Fiction. 4. Domestic fiction. 5. Bildungsromans.

PR9499.4.M35 P58 2017
823'.92—dc23 LC   2016053020

Printed in the United States of America

Arpita

Subhasree

Inaya

1

Disaster came early in Ori's life, at the age of five, the first time he saw his mother die.

Around him was a warm nest of people, people who munched on popcorn, their faces lit up by the reddish yellow light of the fire pit. They looked around, put their arms around him lovingly, their palms covering his eyes, and murmured, "Look away. You don't have to see this." To each other they said, "We should have put him to bed."

They stroked him absently, unable to tear their eyes away from the slow dance of light and shadow on which his mother floated to her death. A few hundred black heads peeped out of the cotton sheets and woollen shawls around their bodies, gazing across the open ground, hypnotized by her pain. His father hugged him, but his arms felt cold. "You're crying?" His voice mocked, sounding as if it was coming from far away, "*Dhur boka!*"

Ori didn't scream. But the world blurred as tears pooled at the corners of his glasses. Nausea gathered in his bowels like thick mist and the heat rose to his skin. In the blurred light, he saw his mother's head slump back as she lay on the ground. She was dead. Her long hair spread on the floor like a still pool of blood. A breath of relief raged through him. He sensed his fever evaporate and his skin turn cold from sweat.

He did not know when he had fallen asleep. His father had grabbed his wrist. "Come"—and led him through the darkness, whispering, "Just hold on to my hand. *Tight korey.*"

They had inched their way under the makeshift wooden structure, through narrow passages veined with electric cables, to the room of white light and giant mirrors. It was the kind of room he would see hundreds of times, all over the country, choked with the smell of wigs and makeup and cotton and silk, charged with the sauciness of women in bras and petticoats smoking cigarettes, the coiffure of Mughal princesses still heaped over their heads.

That night, he had needed to see her. Still heavy with gold jewelry and the rich sari, her hair a black river flowing down her back. She caught sight of his reflection in the long mirror before her, smiled, and came back to life. But she did not turn around. Or leave her seat to take him in her arms.

He stood at the threshold for a long moment. Her smile felt strange, out of place. He had just seen her suffer a life of misery and meet her death with calm, and here she was, smiling, alive, in the greenroom thick with cigarette smoke and sharp with the glare of electric bulbs. His heart leaped with happiness, and a pang of betrayal.

Blinded by the lights and the mirrors, he averted his eyes.

⸙

He was now ten years old, but little-boyhood still crept upon him sometimes, dull gray patches of sweetness and terror. Some memories were animals that would not be buried.

Once upon a time, he had shared the stage with her. It was a long, long time ago, but the memory had stayed with him, like a haunting dream. Sharp metal had clanged over his head; the shine of violence had seeped through his closed eyes. He was a child clad in white, stolen in his sleep for slaughter before a thirsty goddess, saved from murder just as a timely sword clashed with the machete swinging toward his tiny head. It was a play by a very famous poet, in which his mother had played a cruel queen. He was just a baby then, they would tell him later, a baby who hadn't started at the clash of steel. He hadn't cried, as if he were really asleep! What a natural, they had said. But that brave sleep had led to nothing.

The stage drew him like a magnet. Its warm fragrance drove him mad. But his mother did not want him to act. If anyone ever talked about putting him to use in the play, a wailing baby in someone's arms, a child left alone on the streets, she'd laugh it off. *Not him, what an absurd idea!*

She shrugged off each attempt to put him on stage, always with something which looked like indifference.

Except last Thursday.

The theatre stood in the neighbourhood where Beadon Street cut through Central Avenue, a place where the dust of the city mixed with something . . . a breezy fragrance, something strange and sweet. It was a place he passed daily on his way to school, a place barely off the main street and close to his home, less than five minutes on the school bus if the traffic flowed easily. Marking the streets were aged tracks along which doddering trams clanged their way west, all the way to Howrah station and the river at the edge of the city. But that was not why the neighbourhood felt strange.

Evening hung over the place, though it was not yet six. The darkness did not scare him. He was eager to get to the theatre around the corner. This was, he knew, the evening for the full rehearsal, with costumes and music and everything. His mother never took him along to full rehearsals. But he had wandered from the park where he played in the evening. With quiet determination, he had drifted through the snarl of the traffic. He knew these lanes a little—once, he had come here with his mother and her friends in a car, which had left them right in front of the theatre. Today, as he walked on, he caught a whiff of flowers.

He looked around and realized what was different about these roadside stalls selling cigarettes and *paan* leaves. They all sold flowers. Stems of roses and thin garlands of white evening bloomers, jasmine, tuberoses—cold, moist, exquisitely formed blossoms that one saw in weddings as well as funerals. Music played from the tiny transistor radios hidden under the stacks of flowers and chewing tobacco, love songs from Hindi movies, many of them from many, many years ago, crackling on the airwaves in slow, nasal tones.

First, he saw the men—reed thin, in shabby shirts flapping around their bony ribs—wandering the pavements. They looked aimless but worried, as if they had something on their minds but couldn't talk about it. Their bodies arched eagerly toward every passing man, to whom they clung for a few moments, whispering breathless appeals. What were they saying? He saw no merchandise on them, no sachets of chewing tobacco, trays of sliced fruits, or bottles of soda that vendors usually tried to thrust on pedestrians making their way through city neighbourhoods. He glanced at them furtively as he walked. But none of the men looked at him.

Turning into a narrow lane, he saw the women. They stood next to each other in a line along the houses, facing the street in a wriggling, snake-like row. A scattered chain of shiny dresses, fire-red makeup on dark skin, and flowers wreathed around buns and waves of hair. They laughed and nudged each other; some of them stretched out their arms to beckon passersby.

Ori walked past them as quickly as he could, trying to look away. His heart beat wildly. He could not say why. He had thought only children had to stand in line, like he did in school, on the way to prayer in the assembly hall. He didn't know adults could be made to stand that way too.

Almost running now, he suddenly came up right against the theatre. It seemed to tear its way up through the ground, a rugged mass of aged bricks, a giant iron gate. The gate was locked, he knew, but the smaller door next to it was not, and he pushed it open to enter the building. The lobby was half-lit and shadowy; weak music spilled out past the door to the main gallery. Locked and unlit, the little ticket counter on the right looked like an empty cage. On the walls, framed posters of plays glowed in the shadows. The place knotted magic and fear inside his stomach; a dense, wooden kind of fragrance filled his nostrils as he moved toward the door of the auditorium. He tiptoed through the door and stopped short, taking in a strange sight.

The play's male lead was on the stage, alone. He was lightly moving his body to a song playing backstage: "Sunsaabasun." The song to which everybody was dancing that year. The actor wasn't quite dancing, but his movements were close to it. From time to time, he'd pause, flex his wiry muscles at an oblong mirror placed awkwardly in a corner, stare at himself, then start stepping to the music as it picked up the tempo. From across the hall, he looked tiny, a lit-up puppet in shiny clothes. Everybody in that empty hall looked tiny. The few people occupying the front row talked and laughed among themselves. Nobody paid attention to the man on stage.

Suddenly Ori heard his mother's voice. He felt so happy that he wanted to cry. She was right there in the front row. He could see her topknot and a little shimmer of an orange sari. He had not seen that sari before. He didn't know if he should run up to her or call out to her. She tossed back her head and laughed, and talked to her coactors in the voice he knew; it was not her stage voice. And yet the light and the music and the lilt of her laughter made him hesitate. The lit-up stage at the far end of the empty auditorium held him entranced. Slowly a kind of gloom came over him at the thought of his mother playing the lead opposite the prancing, mirror-gazing man with the wiry good looks, twisting his body whimsically to the beat of the racy music. The music stopped and everybody became quiet in preparation for the next scene. The man was gone and Ori saw his mother climb up the steps, ready to play her part.

A shrill voice spoke up right above him, startling him. "And who are you, sweetie?" In the wispy darkness of the hall, the man's strange, drawn-out voice offered a kind of comfort.

Ori turned, looked up. "I'm looking for my mother," he said.

"Of course you are!" The man looked at the stage. "Little boys and girls need their mothers all the time. And who is your mother?"

Shyly he whispered the name.

"What?" The man leaned forward, brought his face close to Ori's mouth. "Can't hear anything."

"Garima Basu," Ori said again, his face growing warm and red.

"Come with me," the man said. "I'll send word to her."

They stepped back into the lobby, where they ran into a couple of young women with whom the man spoke briefly, his voice a strange parody of theirs. Ori followed him into a tiny cubbyhole of a room leading off the lobby. It had just about enough space for a large round table piled high with photocopied sheets. Ori had seen these sheets at home many times. They were from the script of the play his mother was rehearsing. The sheets were filled with handwritten scribbles, the topmost bearing a name written in flowing strokes of ink: Ahin Mullick, Producer.

The man's face, now more visible in the sickly yellow light, was gaunt. His jaws moved constantly and his lips were red from the betel leaves he chewed.

"Good-looking!" Softly, the man's fingers caressed Ori's cheeks. "What a sweet face!" His fingers trailed down and lightly cupped his chin. Ori twitched his nose to balance his glasses, an old habit grown out of the fear that they might slip off.

He was used to this sort of talk. It felt nice too. Under thick glasses, he had myopic eyes that looked dreamy, and his delicate mouth was arched like a pretty girl's. But he disliked his small head, lost under his shock of shiny hair, wet-looking hair. The smallness annoyed him. It made him look too young.

"Let me see something." The man leaned forward.

The fragrance of spiced betel leaves made Ori dizzy. The man removed Ori's glasses. Ori blinked, lost in the haze into which the world suddenly melted away.

"Have you ever acted in a play?" The man gently put the glasses down on the pile of scripts, his gaze still on Ori's face.

Swimming in the shapeless world, Ori felt his heart leap. *He would love to act!* He looked up to the man. The face, once gaunt, was now a patch of shadow. Ori could not speak. He wanted to smile but his lips would not move. He twitched his nose and remembered the glasses were not there.

"Take off your shirt." The man's voice echoed in the tiny room.

Ori's heart jumped to his throat. At ten, he was deeply ashamed of his growing body; he would not sleep shirtless during the hottest of nights. He stepped back a little, away from the man. The man came closer, reached out to touch the collar of his shirt. "I'm older than your father. You can't be shy with me."

He stood limp, letting the man's fingers unbutton his shirt. His ears felt warm and his brain clouded by the intense fragrance of spiced betel leaves. He would not fight a man who wanted him for the stage. He let the man remove all the buttons, even stretched his arms so that the shirt could be eased off his body.

"Very nice complexion." The man looked pleased. "It will glow in the spotlight."

Warmly, his palm lingered on Ori's shoulder, slid along his upper arms. His palm looked dry and bony but felt soft on Ori's skin.

"My mother . . ." he whispered. "She will not let me act." Tremors shot through his body as the man caressed his chest. The palm paused. The man breathed slowly, and Ori felt soft fingers touch his left nipple. Suddenly his life started to seep away slowly through the tiny raw circle on his chest.

But he wanted his skin to glow on the stage. He wanted it badly. "You can. Nobody . . . there is nobody quite like you," said the cloudy form before his naked eyes. "You'd be perfect. Come, put on this shirt." He held out a black silk shirt that looked too large.

"Here." The man turned him sideways and slipped an arm into a sleeve.

As he turned to face the door, his mother appeared on the threshold.

He wanted to curl up, burrow underground. What had she seen? *Nothing*, he wanted to shout. She had seen nothing, heard nothing. He shot up and groped the piles of paper on the table for his glasses, his heart racing. Where were they?

Her body shook with laughter. Liquid, cruel laughter in spasms. For a while, she could not speak.

"You've got to stop, Ahin-da." She was still laughing, though her voice was firm. "He has no time to act."

"Let him put this on." Ahin held out the dark silk shirt. "Just this once. He has the face and the complexion. How old is he?"

The laughter evaporated from her face. Her jaws tightened. Her voice became low. "Just keep him out of this, will you?"

The man wouldn't let go. Was he insane? He insisted, in his girlish voice, that she let him try one rehearsal, just once.

She clasped her son's arm sharply and pulled him out of the room. Then she stepped inside.

"How . . ." Suddenly her voice wilted. "Have you . . ." she whispered, "stopped taking your pills? Again?"

A few people had gathered outside, their eyes shiny.

"Where's your shirt?" she turned to Ori and asked, her eyes stabbing through his naked chest. His nipples felt raw in the clammy air of the corridor, so raw they hurt.

She grabbed his shirt, lying on the table with the ribboned scripts, and flung it out at him. The shirt landed on Ori's face, hiding the strange yellow eyes of the man who had wanted him so badly, for the stage.

2

His mother acted in plays. He carried that knowledge like a wound. He was afraid to nurse it lest others noticed. But pain swirled around it, and flies buzzed. Everybody thought it was wrong of his mother to leave the home every evening, delicately dressed and fragrant. Evenings spent in the glare and noise of rehearsals, shows on Thursdays, Saturdays, and Sundays in the local theatre halls. Bright-lit evenings and the warm, perfumed smell of greenrooms and the rowdy energy of men and women whose limbs swam in the lilt of music. It created bitterness at home, great dark swathes of it.

They tried to hide the wound but it spilled over everywhere. His grandmother, his Mummum never mentioned it; she nursed it in silence. His Aunt Rupa muttered about it, grating words inside her mouth.

He remembered the men who used to dash into their house back when he was little. They were men who smelled of wild grass and cigarette smoke, with stubble on their cheeks that hurt when they kissed him. "Uri Uri Bubbah!" they would whistle. They would tickle him cruelly and swing him in the air; he would see the blue sky below him and the bannister of the balcony above and shriek in fear. But they never stayed long. Sometimes they just crowded the landing of the staircase, thickening the air with smoke and song and strange cuss words while waiting for his mother to come out, dressed and ready for her rehearsal. Inside the house, the maids lowered their voices to a whisper and a cloud fell across Rupa's face. Sometimes Rupa's maid answered the door and called Ori's mother: "Didi, your *babus* are here." Ori hated the way she said it. He wanted to run out of the house, leave with his mother, with the wild and smoky men.

But these days, his mother left the house alone. Sometimes a car came to pick her up, but no one ever stepped out of it.

The smell of violence always floated in the air. Back when he was seven or eight, he remembered an old man who sometimes came to see his grandmother. Mr. Tarafdar, a retired barrister who had worked with his grandfather. Even in his late seventies, he had the manner of the stern English magistrates you saw in movies. Ori's grandmother never forgot to cover her head with the end of her sari, pulling it low over her forehead, like a shy newlywed before a stranger.

"I've never really cared for plays, Manashi," Mr. Tarafdar had said one evening in his rich voice that filled up the room. "But my daughter and son-in-law dragged me off to see *Bar-badhu* at Rangmahal, and what can I tell you? Your *bouma*, Garima, she is magic on stage. Pure magic, that's what she is."

Bar-badhu was a funny play where a man and a woman pretended to be married but in fact they were not; apparently the woman did this for money, play wife to men who needed to look like they were married. Garima was such a natural, such a genius in the role of the fake wife, so full of tears and laughter and domestic bliss, that you forgot that you were watching a play inside a play. The old man had sipped at his tea noisily as he spoke, his aged eyes dreamy, and Ori's heart had swelled with so much pride that it hurt.

But moments after Mr. Tarafdar left the house, a hiss of words between Rupa and his grandmother struck a slap on his cheeks. The barrister was such a dirty old man, they said. Ori had stared at his grandmother's stricken face, the sari-anchal slipping off her head, and he heard Rupa chew out bitter words against the shameless Mr. Tarafdar, and slowly, Ori's anger had swelled—against the old barrister who had watched his mother on stage, and then, against his mother. Great, fuming burst of fury that had made his eyes well up.

It was wrong of her to pretend to be someone else's wife. They hated it, his aunt and his grandmother. The maids giggled with strange, starstruck eyes. He remembered the photograph that had appeared once in a newspaper, a close-up shot of his mother's face and that of another man, looking at each other with a strange kind of fear in their eyes. White and intense, the faces did not seem fully human. But it was a picture from a play he had seen her rehearse, where she was married to a young and handsome landowner, a rich zamindar who drank whisky all the time and lost his estate. The spotlight and the makeup had made their faces scary as the zamindar and his suffering wife looked at each other, lost in a kind of fear that made you shiver as you looked at the picture. Everyone at home hated the picture, throwing away the day's newspaper like it was touched with disease; he had seen the maids pick up the rubbished page, smooth out the creases, gaze at the photograph with a shine in their eyes, whisper to each other.

❧

Some evenings he tagged along with his mother to her rehearsals, full of anxious actors and musicians. Fidgety, nervous people who pinched his cheeks and ruffled his hair and then forgot about him. All except the hairdresser, Pallabi, who shadowed his mother wherever she went and seemed to secretly wait for him to arrive. She smiled and sometimes winked at him but never said anything. Ori liked her but he did not like it when she winked; he always turned his face away.

Quickly he became invisible again, free to wander along the corridors outside or stay inside to see young actors try to get jealous or sad. Or to read a book he'd brought along. He could follow the rehearsed lines far better than most could imagine, and the most intense scenes, repeated endlessly, took on strange colours in his mind. But he rarely spoke. Quickly the actors forgot about him and got on with their rehearsal.

Every time his mother came back from a rehearsal with Ori in tow, a hushed silence fell at home. As if everyone were holding their breaths. And then the questions began to trickle, voices dropping so low that they were mere whispers. Where did his mother go for the rehearsal? Which part of the city?

Did you see a lot of men there? Were they young like your Baba, or old men with no hair?

Sometimes their words burnt a hole through his heart.

One night after dinner as he was sitting on his grandmother's bed and talking to her, his Aunt Rupa had walked into the room to take care of her last chores for the evening. A woman from the neighbourhood walked in with her, a friend of the family whose raspy voice often echoed throughout the house. As the two women pottered around the room tidying up stray ends, Ori's grandmother fell into silence.

"Ori?" Rupa asked. "How was the rehearsal this evening?"

He didn't know what to say.

"That play is a classic," Rupa chattered on, pouring water into his grandmother's glass and covering it with a small porcelain saucer. Everybody agreed that Rupa was the working nerve center of the house. She was the widow of Ori's uncle, his father's only brother, a man with weak lungs who had died when Ori was a toddler. Rupa was a dark and angular woman with a face nobody glanced at a second time in this family of beautiful, fair-skinned people. Briskly she would go around the house making sure none of the maids shirked their duties or filched a chipped coin lying forgotten under the bed. Her fingertips understood money; she worked all day counting crisp notes and shiny coins behind an iron cage in the local branch of the State Bank. No maid in this house could get away with fooling her about change due back from the shopkeepers.

Her voice tightened whenever she spoke about Ori's mother.

"But it has only one female character," her friend said absently, her bangles clinking against each other. "Perfect for an amateur group in a corporate house."

"Naturally they had to hire a professional actress," Rupa said as she arranged the old woman's nighttime pills on a little dish. "No woman in the office would act. And certainly not in such a role."

Ori's grandmother looked out of the window. She was the most beautiful old woman Ori had seen. A marble statue in widow's white. She looked lonely. Gazing at her deep-wrinkled hands, Ori's heart ached with love.

She was an ancient, regal woman, his Mummum, clean and fragrant with a fresh-mint smell. She loved to read and tell stories, loved to recite hymns in Sanskrit in her trembling old-woman voice.

Rupa shot a glance at Ori. "Garima is the only woman in that play, isn't she?"

Ori wanted his grandmother to look inside, say something. Urgently.

"I've lost count of the number of times I've read the novel," Rupa's friend said dreamily. "My heart's in my mouth whenever I get to the scene where she seduces her brother-in-law." She paused, holding her breath. "A boy half her age."

The night air breezed through the window. The old woman's jaws tightened.

Rupa left the room with her friend. But the air would not thaw. Slowly Mummum turned to him, her ancient eyes unblinking. "What was your mother wearing today?" she asked.

Bewildered, he still knew better than to tell the truth: that his mother, the only woman that evening in a loud group of men, had ditched her staid cotton sari to put on a skin-hugging salwar for the rehearsals. Got to live the character and move free, she had said.

Sweat thickened on the bridge of his nose. He grimaced, worrying his glasses would slip off. For a moment, he was silent.

"Why?" Suddenly he had turned to stare at her. "She was wearing a sari. The cotton one the colour of *pista*."

His father had no questions for him. Ori wished he did sometimes, for that would have made him an ordinary man, not a wounded god. A beautiful god, tall and pale with chiseled features, who had once loved the theatre. His Baba, the man whose pale and delicate features, everybody said, had given shape to his own, the same, slightly crooked nose and the same arched lips. A man who must have been happy once. He loved to recite the long Bangla poems, the epics, and the crisp, witty satires, and to sing Tagore songs in his rich and generous voice. There was a time when he loved to see his wife act, loved to see her rehearse her roles. But as bitterness thickened at home, he stopped going to watch her plays. Sometimes he would still come to pick her up from her rehearsals and they would return home together. But he would not come inside to meet the other actors, laugh and joke with them. Not anymore. Ori would step out to find him pacing the sidewalk, smoking in silence. Sometimes they took a long walk home. Sometimes they would take a rickshaw and Ori had to squeeze between his parents. They didn't talk much on the way; sometimes Ori's mother would laugh about something that happened at the rehearsal. But his father would say nothing.

These days, he rarely went out in the evenings. Often Ori found him in his room, tucked into bed, with the lights turned out. It frightened Ori to see night drop so early on him. Sometimes he wondered if he was sick. His aunt and her neighbourhood friends stung bee-like whenever they could: absently, they wondered if Garima would be back in time for dinner, liquid laughter spilling over their lips as memory came back to them, without any warning, and they recalled that her group was now in a faraway city for a performance.

Ori treasured his nights in his grandmother's room, despite its climate of intrigue, far from the hot vapor of anger in his parents' bedroom as they locked themselves in after dinner. Only with Mummum was he safe. *No one else.* More and more, his parents spoke to each other in a heated whisper, slashing at each other, unable to keep the acid from dripping through the door. Ori shuddered at the smell of his parents' bedroom, the sharp smell of hatred. But sometimes he closed his eyes and saw places that were really far away, far from the burnt air of the city. Places that held happiness and kept it safe. Towns where he half-remembered holidaying with his parents, holidays, he heard, had been happy. A white hotel in Puri where they gave him a glass of buffalo milk every morning. A foggy bungalow in Kalimpong that belonged to a doctor who was his father's friend. His aunt's house where they vacationed every year, a windy palace in Hoogly, with water hyacinths clogging the ponds and fire trucks resting near the house like tiny, rust-encrusted buildings, a strangely soothing sight.

3

People liked to talk about their house where Ori lived. The yellow house in the winding lane, with walls crowded with fresh and faded election graffiti, the palm and the lion and the hammer-sickle-star painted over it. But the neighbours couldn't stop talking about the lives contained in the house.

The old widow of the Barrister Sahib still had a touch of rose on her wrinkled skin and the dream of a home where women spoke in hushed voices and had their eyes glued to the floor while speaking. But more than ten years had passed since the Barrister Sahib's death and no one else seemed to remember those times. People talked and laughed loudly whenever they felt like and the crows on the windowsills cawed more harshly than ever before.

"This is no longer a home," the old widow liked to say. "It has become a slum!"

It made people angry. Bad bile flowed in strange directions, tainting everything. Why did Mummum shout at Shruti all the time? She was her granddaughter too, Rupa's only child, a girl without a father. And why did Shruti always speak to Mummum in that mean, biting way?

One Bijoya Dashami, Ori remembered, Shruti, then in Class Six, had asked Mummum if she could go down and stand outside to watch the lights of the last day of Durga Pujo. It was a massive carnival out there, with cavalcades of people carrying the icon of the goddess and her family to the Ganga River, a ten minutes' walk from their place, where the clay images would be sunk in the water. She just had to go, all her friends were there at the crossing of the main street where the trucks were passing slowly with the giant images and beating drums and the dancing neon lights. Everybody was there and she wasn't going to miss it. No way.

Mummum's face had darkened. Then she had pointed to little Ori. "Take him with you."

"Him?" Shruti grimaced like Ori was a small animal with a bad odour. "What will he do there?"

"Whatever you will," Mummum said coldly. "You want him to stay back at home while you go and watch the carnival?"

Shruti rolled her eyes around in disgust but, in the end, ran downstairs dragging Ori by the hand. Ori tripped and fell and she twisted his wrist so hard that he wanted to cry. But he'd held back the tears; he really wanted go with Shruti to watch the carnival of the Pujo *bisarjan* go by. Out there, they had forgotten about everything, it had been so splendid, the lights and the drums and the booming music and the people swaying and dancing like mad, and Shruti had found her friends and they had all shrieked in glee and Ori had stood there, terrified and spellbound. He had lost count of the number of images that had passed—ten, fifteen, twenty— the fairytale design of lights on the massive trucks, castles and dinosaurs and monuments and cricketers, and firecrackers thrown around like blazing confetti, and he'd had no idea how long they had stood there till he needed to peepee. He could go to the bathroom on his own but there was no bathroom here and no place to peepee either with the lights and the people and the screaming, and he was too scared to ask Shruti who was frantic laughing with her friends and had luckily forgotten that Ori was even there. But the peepee did not go away and just bloated up inside him and kept nudging, till it started to hurt and he just looked up and said: "Peepee!" Nobody heard anything and he couldn't hear his own voice either in the middle of all the boom boom, and he tried to make the peepee go away but it wouldn't, and so he said again after a few minutes: "Peepee!" Nothing happened. Nobody took notice but neither did the peepee go away so soon he peepeed in his pants and the trickle along his legs felt terrible but it was also very nice to feel free again inside.

They returned home a bit later and on their way back Ori said, "I need to go peepee." He wasn't sure why he had said that as he had already done what he had needed to do but he still felt that he should say it. But Shruti was in a better mood, and kinder, and all she said was: "You're a bloody pain but anyway we're home and go run to the bathroom."

But they knew it at home. The peepee had dried on his legs but his pants were wet. Rupa laughed and took him away to get him cleaned but he saw Mummum's face grow cloudy. She told him nothing but spoke to Shruti in a dead kind of a voice.

"Such fun it was, wasn't it? You wouldn't have noticed if he was run over by a truck!"

"What?" Shruti had shouted. "He never told me anything. I had no idea he needed to go to the bathroom."

Ori kept quiet. He had actually tried to tell her a few times, but it was best not to say anything about that now.

"Standing on the streets with a bunch of rotten girls." Mummum's voice fell to a whisper. "Giggling without a care in the world. Do you know what you look like out there?"

Quickly Rupa had pulled Shruti away. Rupa was just as strict as Mummum and they were usually on the same side, but Rupa loved her daughter, loved her very much. Shruti had turned and stuck her tongue out at her grandmother but Rupa had bluntly dragged her out of the room.

His Mummum had strange rules but she practiced them with such a force that quickly you forgot everything else and the rule smoothly became part of your normal life. Suddenly Shruti could not go out alone anymore. Twelve or thirteen, how old was she exactly? Ori didn't quite remember. He was too young himself; Shruti was seven years older than he was. But they were weird rules and continued to puzzle him. Someone had to accompany Shruti whenever she stepped out on the streets, and if no one was around, she was to take Ori along. Why? Just a few months back, Shruti could stand by the door all by herself and watch the monkey man's shows and laugh and shriek as much as she wanted. She was older now; and she couldn't go out alone? What happened if she laughed on the streets?

He loved being able to go places with Shruti, but Shruti simmered in rage whenever he tagged along. He hoped desperately that she would not begin to hate him. They had grown up like siblings in that house, entangled together in spite of the difference in their ages. But now the sight of him drove her mad. It was nice to run out of home together to buy spicy *ghoogni* or *chaat* at the main street crossing, and she never forgot to ask them to make his portion without chillis, but she wasn't so nice when he tagged along with her to the home of a school friend in the neighbourhood to ask about a class she had missed. Her friends laughed and whispered about him and Shruti was angry the whole time, and said really, really mean things if he tried to say anything. It was just as well that she wasn't allowed to go out very often outside of school and small errands or else she might have done something bad to him, knocked him down or scratched out his eyes.

But Ori learnt how to make himself invisible. It was quite easy. His mind wandered often while Shruti and her friends laughed about weird stuff at school, things that were not funny at all, and people soon forgot he was there. As the years went by and Shruti moved beyond Class Ten, he became one of her habits, a weird kind of habit according to her friends, but then they also stopped noticing him. By then he was six and could take care of his bathroom needs on his own and was no bother if he tagged along. Mostly he was left alone with a book of comics while the girls did a strange kind of homework, giggling and whispering angrily and then shaking with laughter again. But he liked it best when it was just he and Shruti and no one else, such as when they went together to offer prayer at the Saraswati Pujo just outside their house and they made weird voices and made fun of everybody at home. It was hard to believe that she could go out anywhere without him tagging along.

⁂

Things began to feel different when Shruti started college. Now a first-year student, she trashed Mummum's house rule easily, but Ori, now in Class Five, still went out with her sometimes. Sometimes even when she went to college in Park Street, a bit of a bus ride away from their house. But college was a big and strange place and it scared Ori a little. The grounds were huge and flooded with rough, jostling people of all kinds and full of cigarette smoke and the kind of loudness he had never heard among Shruti's girlfriends who lived close to their home.

There were a lot of boys, more boys than girls, boys who smoked cigarettes nonstop and scratched at their grimy skin restlessly, spit out gum and *paan parag* juice wherever they felt like. They were funny and puzzling but also mean; unlike his mother's actor friends, they did not care at all that Ori was a child, did not, in fact, care about him at all. They would poke him around a bit, offer to buy him a balloon just to see him redden a little. His pale skin made his emotions easily visible to the world. But quickly they would forget that he was there. He listened to them breathlessly and ached to say something, something smart and funny, but could never think of anything. They talked about the bitterness of bloodspill over student elections and the cloud of crack dealers around college. Such times he had to keep shut, stay so quiet that they forgot he was there.

That afternoon they were talking about boys who visited prostitutes. Boys or men, what were they? Smooth boy-men whom they admired a little and also hated a little. There were the Anglo-Indian prostitutes around the Indian Museum near Park Street who sneaked out in the evening. And then there was Sonagachhi farther north, the largest red-light district in town, such a filmy-type place. You couldn't walk in the lanes without the men hissing all over you, "Fresh meat, babu, just arrived last week. Gori and a virgin. Whip me if she's more than sixteen," foulmouthed Abir crooned in a mock-Bihari accent.

"I went to Sonagachhi last Thursday," Ori said suddenly, his voice down to a whisper.

The silence was so thick that he heard the lub-dub of his own heart.

"The girls stand in a row, their faces are painted and they tie strings of white flowers on their hair." He couldn't stop. His glasses twitched on his nose. "They laugh and jab at each other with their elbows."

Abir found his tongue before the others. "What the *fuck*," he spat, "were you doing there?"

"I had gone to look for Ma."

"You were looking in the wrong place." Abir's eyes seared through Ori's. "She's business class."

What? As Ori tried to make sense of the words, he heard Shruti's sharp voice. "You bastard! You mention my aunt just one more time and I'll rip your tongue out."

Darkness shadowed Shruti's copper-coloured face when provoked. She loved her aunt and got sore about her easily. Love made her look different, shinier and sweatier. Ori's ears buzzed and heat raged around them. What did she see in Abir anyway? He wasn't even that handsome or anything, just a street bully who had dropped out of college after a year's shot at an ordinary B.Com from some godforsaken college. That's what Rupa always said.

Abir's right hand curled around Shruti's shoulders. Her back stiffened. She tried to wriggle free. Abir didn't care; lazily, he started caressing the back of her neck, the tiny stretch of bare flesh above her top.

She glared at Ori. "So that's where you went wandering off after school on Thursday?"

"I saw the women on my way to Ruby Theatre," Ori said. "The men too. They were running after everybody." Dumb anger spread through his body at the way Abir caressed the back of Shruti's neck, as if it was a soft toy he liked to play with. Ori wanted to smash his fist at his face.

Srinjoy asked, "How did you know you were passing a brothel?"

"Especially since this was your first time," someone piped. "Or was it?"

"Shut your trap, JD!" Shruti snapped. "Shows *your* class."

"I didn't understand at first," Ori mused. "I had no idea what they were selling.

"It was strange the way the girls stood in a line." A frown creased his face. "As if they were in a parade or something."

"Why the . . . ?" Shruti bit her lips. "Does Mummum know that you went there alone?" Shruti asked.

"Mummum?" Ori was suddenly struck with terror. "I wouldn't be here if she knew!" A nervous laugh escaped his lips at the thought of his grandmother coming to know what he had been up to.

"Why is he here anyway?" Abir mumbled.

An electric current seemed to kiss Ori's insides as Abir glanced at him. The guy's spindly fingers were now under Shruti's top. They ran gentle circles on her back, tugged gently at her bra straps.

Turning away, he told the others about the funny man. The man with a singsongy voice. Ahin Mullick, his mother had said, was happy, with a mouthful of laughter and betel leaves, only when he took his pills. But sometimes when he didn't, his shirt looked blood-sprinkled, paan-juice spilt through his mouth, and he did things that warmed your skin, made it flush.

"What the fuck?" Shruti whistled, her voice raw, eyes wide. "He took your shirt off?"

It *was* odd. Ahin-da! People rarely noticed when he came or went. He called himself a producer! Of a ghost troupe in that ghost playhouse where he lived, a sad house of the dead. A strange ache filled Ori's head as he thought of the man's fingers rubbing his nipple, coating it with shame. He didn't want to think about it.

Shruti was quiet again, but Ori knew when something clouded her mind.

"Sicko!" a voice hissed.

He was a sick man. Ahin-da. The red-lipped man of restless, betel-chewing jaws whose eyes had sparkled at the skin of his young shoulders. What kind of illness was it?

"If you want better," Abir said, "what the fuck are you doing in a theatre around the corner from a row of whores?" His right arm curled around Shruti's waist and nudged its way under her top.

"Don't talk about stuff you don't understand." Shruti's voice was cold. "These are hard times for the theatre. People have to be versatile to survive."

"Versatile in what sort of skills?" Abir snorted loudly. He pulled his hand out from under Shruti's top, lit his cigarette, and blew out a swirl of smoke like a steam engine picking up speed.

>✧✧<

Abir hated him. Ori knew that. Abir did not try to hide it. It was a muted hatred, soft around the edges, but with a vicious heart that spat out often. The spit clung to him even when Ori tried not to think about Abir. Sometimes the fear made him angry. The guy might wear shiny locket chains and stretch out on the green benches of Saint Xavier's, but he was just some lowlife from some dingy lane near the big railway station. Some slum perhaps. He had that kind of spit and curse aggression. And the windbag knowledge of everything that belonged to the ancient lanes of north Calcutta.

He reminded Ori of the jobless young men in loose pyjamas and rubber flip-flops in their neighbourhood, who played carom on street corners all day and organized strikes and lockouts for the local wing of the Communist Party. He was even thick with the mean guys in their neighbourhood, and lounged around the tea stalls and boys' clubs, waiting to meet Shruti whenever she could slip out of home.

"A child growing up, watching his mother play a different role every evening," he would say while blowing smoke rings like the hulking men at the neighbourhood tea shops, "is obscene."

It drove Shruti crazy. Her flaring anger excited Abir. He seemed to enjoy her threats, and her anger got lost in the pleasure he got from them.

"God," she would say with disgust, "you sound like my mother! And the Party thugs who want to clean up the neighbourhood."

"Who would have thought the Party thugs wanted to sweep clean playhouses?" Srinjoy wondered. His parents owned the flat on Wood Street often plundered by his classmates. "What would Marxism be without the theatre?" It was the kind of thing Srinjoy couldn't understand, and he was a really, really smart guy. He could party like a rock star but everybody in Saint Xavier's knew he would breeze through the management exams and land in one of the top business schools.

Why couldn't Shruti like him more than she liked that slum guy Abir?

"North Calcutta is not your Theatre Road or Ballygunje," Shruti said. "You don't know how everybody butts into each other's lives."

"Big deal," JD snorted. "Everybody knows Raj Kapoor screwed all his heroines."

"You south Calcutta types don't know the north at all," Shruti sighed. "Some people still think theatre is the place people go to sniff dirt."

"That's crazy!" Srinjoy said. "This is 1985 in case you didn't notice."

Abir stripped the cellophane off a new pack of cigarettes.

"Have you guys seen these north Calcutta halls?" Suddenly, his dead-cold eyes fixed on Ori. "The kind of plays they put on? Fat old aunties dancing in colourful panties to Bollywood numbers."

An eerie violence in his voice silenced everybody. Shruti looked away abruptly.

"Stay away from your aunt," Abir said. "That woman is bad news."

"Fuck you!" Shruti flared up. "You know nothing about her. *Nothing.* She does all kinds of plays. She's a talented group theatre artist. Sometimes you have to do different things to put a career together."

"A career in what?" Abir's tossed-out words were like ashes flicked off his cigarettes, uncaring of whose skin they singed. Shruti suddenly looked tired; the sudden flashes of heat in her brain at his thoughtless cruelty had exhausted her. In the end, silence descended upon the group like a black rain cloud while Ori sat with his head in his palms, cupping a throbbing pain.

4

Once upon a time, the familiarity of his neighbourhood was a deep comfort to Ori. There were lanes fringed with familiar shops from which faces smiled at him as he walked. It was more than a neighbourhood constructed from bricks and mortar; it was a *para*, a mesh of lanes and voices that chattered with one another tirelessly. But these days, he avoided the front gate of their house. He didn't like to face the neighbours. He wanted to hide from their keen glances.

Their memories brought up a dull pain. There was a strange spark in their eyes when they spoke of his parents in love. It left people hot and bothered those days. A boy and a girl strolling the crooked streets of north Calcutta together, close enough to breathe on each other, for several years before they married, streets noisy with gossip and the violence of young Naxalite men being chased and shot by the police. Densely honeycombed with people and houses, these streets had too much to talk about. Scattered pairs of eyes gazed out at the streets all day, the women through the bent mullions of the windows, the jobless men from the ledges and steps outside their homes where they lounged all day. They missed nothing. Sounds and smells told them what was cooking in their neighbour's kitchen every day, and the wind carried words from one house to another.

"Your father," cackled aunties with betel-stained teeth, "was a handful those days, a smooth-talking charmer. The Barrister Saheb's spoilt brat!" Delightfully, the women spat out betel blood. "Cheeky to step out of that house and stroll through the streets with a girl."

Nowadays Ori slipped in and out of the house through the back door. The unclean entry. A frail brown door lined with moss, so weather-beaten that it felt like a reed curtain. It opened onto a narrow, winding strip of unpaved earth called *jomadar goli*—the sweeper's alley. On Mondays and Fridays, the sweeper, a man from an untouchable caste, would slip in through the door and follow the maid who poured water across the bathroom floor from a careful untouchable distance. Fiercely he rubbed his mop and broom across the tiles of the bathrooms.

Ori came to love the narrow, unpaved alley outside the door, the thin strip of reddish earth between moss-covered walls of old houses. High above, pigeons had built an ancient colony. As he walked the red earth, he heard their drowsy hum, trapped in the silence of the lane, punctured only by the flapping of wings and the jostling bodies of birds too lazy to fly. He walked through the deserted alley, until the reddish alley opened out into a small park.

The knot of neighbours lazing in the park made him restless. He felt they were all waiting for him. They waited there all day for him to walk out so that they could whisper among themselves. He sneaked past them quickly and melted into the main thoroughfare, a place of heartwarming chaos, where he felt tiny, near invisible, his life swallowed up by the giant swirls of dust left in the trail of the thundering buses.

He remembered a time when he accompanied his father daily and hung around tea stalls as his father smoked and chatted with his friends. Sometimes the memories lingered, like images on stirred water, and as they broke away he realized that they seemed to be from such a long time ago. His father was now a stranger who always looked sleepy, a stranger with red-rimmed eyes who had forgotten that he had a son.

His father was easy to love. He had the sunlit good looks that ran in that family of fallen gentry, and a wide smile that drew you in like a hug. He loved people wildly and gave himself away all the time, whether to nurse a sick neighbour or to pick a fight about cricket at the roadside stalls. Shruti still called him Tata, only half-remembering that he was the one who had taught baby Shruti to wave 'ta ta,' to people who were about to leave. To his aged mother, he was still the baby boy with divine curls. But he could also be a dangerous baby. He liked to grab his fun by the hair and shake it hard till everybody cried.

Sometimes when his father came home late, his sweat stank of alcohol and he took forever to tear a piece of *ruti* at dinner into bite-sized morsels, his elbow constantly slipping off the table. "I hate your breath," Ori's mother would whisper. "Don't you come close to me!" Nobody had ever talked to him like that before. He looked at her with his red eyes but said nothing. But soon he found ways of shutting out her voice. There were those pills that put him to sleep. There were plenty lying around the house, bent and crushed silver foils, and he reached for them whenever he could. The little pills brought him down every time, crumpled and lost. In a few years' time, the man who loved nothing better than going out and hugging the world spent much of his time forgetting it.

The more she spent her evenings away from home, the easier it was for him to sleep away his own evenings. The more she found him lost, the more she was gone.

⁂

The sweetshop was just around the corner from their house. Its owner was a large, sweet-tongued man who sat in his shop dressed in a white kurta all day, watching over the rows of sweetmeats in the glass boxes—the fried, syrup-soaked *mishti* at the bottom, the milky white *sandesh* on top. He addressed passersby in a cloying manner. Most of them were locals, who stopped by, especially in the evenings, to pick up something. People craved his red yogurt in little clay bowls, and the creamy *rosomalai* was famous throughout north Calcutta. Everybody knew he was a bit of a cheat and often tampered with his weights, but nobody could stay away from his sweets.

That day, he had called Ori from the street.

"Coming back from school, eh?" His eyes shone. "You must be starving!"

Ori tried to smile but did not speak. He didn't know this man well. He was hungry, and stopping at a shop where a permanent sugary aroma hung over everything, it did not feel quite right. He wanted to walk away, but the man would not let him. He ordered his assistant to offer him a leafy plate of crumbly white sandesh. "Eat up," he said. "Time to grow tall and strong!"

"My hands are dirty." He did not know how else to refuse. Sweat gathered between his glasses and the bridge of his nose. His face twitched. But the man would not let go. He led Ori to a sink in the corner of the shop, and pointed to the tiny cake of soap next to it.

Ori stood there and ate the sandesh, the flies dancing in lazy arcs over the glass-encased sweets around him. The pangs of his afternoon hunger slowly wilted in the heat and humidity coming off the street before and the gaze of passing pedestrians. The sandesh were delicious, and as he chewed on each piece and felt them melt in his mouth, he suffered pain, the pain of glorious taste enjoyed not in the cool shadow of his home but in the yellow heat of the streets, listening to the rickshaw pullers cry out to clear their way.

"Is your mother home today?" the shop owner asked, handing Ori a clay pot with deep-fried sweets floating in syrup. He nodded a no, his mouth full. "She's out all evening, isn't she?" Under the double attack of sweets and questions, his head felt muddled, and he chewed for a long time so that he didn't have to talk. But the man waited patiently till Ori could chew no more. "Sometimes," he mumbled. "No one to feed you after you come home from school?" The man stared at him with large, sweaty eyes.

The question slid past him the first day, but when on the third day the whole event repeated itself, freezing again on the same question, the sweets felt like tiny, hard pebbles between his teeth. *No one to feed you?* Ori looked up from the clay pot, his fingers dripping with syrup. A wave of nausea came over him, triggered by the cloying smell of sugar and cottage cheese thick in the air, the sight of the balls of condensed milk in rows and the sticky whiteness of the man's kurta-covered paunch. He wanted to run, but did not wish to offend the kind man who had more questions waiting, if his mother was late every night. Was his father left alone at home? The man knew it all. "She comes back late," Ori mumbled. "After I've gone to sleep." He smiled weakly and swallowed the mishti, unchewed; they went down his throat like tasteless blobs. He stepped out quickly and walked home. He hated sweets.

He was a kind man, the sweetshop owner. There was affection in his voice. They were all kind to him. He turned warm with guilt for not talking to them properly, for running away from them.

※

The next morning, on his way to school, he saw his mother's name plastered on walls all along the winding length of the lane. It was splashed in red and white on patches of flimsy paper pasted on the facades of houses crowded with election graffiti and posters for ice cream. *The Firebird*. The play by a Frenchman whose name Ori could not pronounce, staged in Bengali by one of the theatre groups in the city. They were going to perform soon in a local playhouse.

His mother was playing a key character. Her name was printed loud and bold on each poster, red and white on flimsy paper, something a child might have made in an art class. Walking rapidly, he felt a surge of happiness. He paused before a house and inspected one poster, pasted across the closed shutter of a shop. The paper was stretched thin across the shutter's uneven wood, its rough grains ripped through the large letters of the title. He touched the letters softly; a pang of love shot through his heart. The paper was flimsy, like a page from a cheap newspaper. He looked around, warm around the ears. Had anybody seen him?

The Firebird was also pasted around the rusted metal of lampposts, the flapping wings of the sketched bird hanging broken and torn across the pole, right next to pamphlets for secretarial courses, schools for toddlers, the graffiti of protest against rising prices.

Advertising happened here in the open air, on walls where people aimed their phlegm and piss.

Ori's eyes kept going back to the letters that formed his mother's name. The playful font hugged rough surfaces, round and flat, blazing into a boldness that overshadowed all the other names, the director's and the playwright's, even the flaming bird that had morphed into the letters of the play's title.

But her name was bare. In red and white, the spiky letters screamed for the eyes of passersby, loudly.

How loudly? The evening revealed. That evening, Shruti felt the sudden need to talk to Abir. It was a Sunday and everybody was home. A whole day with her family was bad enough for Shruti to start missing the sound of Abir's voice by the time it was early evening. But she did not like to call him from their home phone. Home was a crazy mess of a place, where the conversation was always killed by her mother walking into the middle of it while the maids shouted for more frying oil in the background. Everybody watched and heard you the whole time. Most of all Mummum who missed nothing even though she didn't understand the English or the coded, quick-fire Bangla Shruti murmured into the phone. To Mummum, people were like breed dogs. Girls from good families never laughed loudly while talking to men, not even on the phone. Shruti would much rather walk over to the phone booth at the para beauty parlor. Did Ori want to come along? Of course he did.

As Shruti entered the little glass enclosure to make her call, he sat on a small stool outside. The employees of the beauty parlor stood at the entrance, smoking and laughing among themselves. Ori listened to the slippery words fly back and forth between them as he watched Shruti's lips, the sound and meaning of her words lost to him behind the sheet of glass. *If she could provide the right kind of massage to the right kind of men.* One of the boys winked at a girl. *She could treble her earnings with the tips.* The girl grimaced; laughter crackled in the air. Behind the glass, he could see Shruti run her fingers through her hair as she spoke rapidly into the receiver. *The doctor from Salt Lake, his eyes are glued to your jugs the whole time you give him a head massage.* Shruti had paused, and was now listening, clutching the phone receiver to her ear, with a frown on her face. *Rub him with your boobs and he'll slip you a fifty!*

The owner of the parlor, a small middle-aged man, stepped out through the door. Suddenly the air cooled and the voices hushed. The man's mouth was crinkled up in disgust. The shadow of a figure had stepped out with him, a sickly, sheepish-looking boy not more than twelve, with a messy bundle of sheets in his hands.

"Harish, get this *bhenchod* out of here," the owner said, with a dismissive wave of his hand. "The fucker's wasted all the posters for the new weekend packages."

Harish was the man who'd been holding forth on new ways of pleasing the men who came to the parlor for massages. He whacked the sickly boy hard on the head, sending him reeling several feet away. "Lost them, has he?" Harish barked. "Cut his meals for the week and we'll get the money back."

"You're a bigger idiot than he is," the owner shouted. "Do you know how much the printing costs were? We can starve him for six months and not get anything back," the owner grunted at the boy. "I've said this I don't know how many times. Choose the spots well and stick them up nicely." The boy tried to melt to the wall. "Dickhead puts all of them up together last evening and now they're plastered over by some other shit!"

"The seenema posters," the boy said in a choked voice. "They took up all the spots."

"You're nuts to give him the posters! Bloody illiterate peasant!"

"You really have to hunt for the good spots here. The bloody tutorial centers come up with a bunch every week and plaster over everything you put up."

"Some bloody shampoo had cleaned out all the spots last week."

"The seenema posters," the frightened boy repeated hoarsely. "The seenema posters were all over the place."

"You can't fight the cinema posters. Way too much muscle."

"Way too much bare skin," Harish reminded them. "Who's going to tear his eyes away from those yummy tummies to read about weekend deals for hairdressing and neck massage?"

"Boss, why don't you spice up our ads a bit? *Intimate massage for real men*—how about that?"

"And make Sonali pose in her bra and panty." Harish winked at the girl, who stuck her tongue out. "People will stop staring at a wet Sridevi dancing in the rain!"

"And then all go to jail?" the owner grunted. "Don't know why I waste my time talking to you potheads. Anyway . . ." He pulled out a large, thin sheet of paper, a poster torn off the walls. "It's not a cinema at all, some play at Angan Theatre next month."

Behind the glass, sparks of laughter lit up Shruti's face. Ori knew they were all watching him, the men and women of the beauty parlor, watching the redness spread like cancer on his skin, the warmth creeping up his ears.

"*The Firebird*," the owner held up the poster. "7th July, Sunday, at Angan Theatre."

Ori knew that the bird's wings were torn in uneven halves, slashed all the way to the credits, gouging out some of the names, now a mess of dried glue and dust. One name more than any other. Of course they all knew him by face. Why was Shruti taking so long? When would they go home?

"Whatever. Cinema, theatre. The bastards go all out. They'd plaster over the stray dogs if they could."

Ori wanted to get up, touch the torn poster. Caress its wound, soothe it, take it away. He wanted to heal the torn wings of the firebird. *It's mine,* he wanted to scream.

The owner had spread out the poster, holding the torn halves together. He was looking at it intently.

How could the sickly boy tear it down? Which one was it? The one that had been pasted around the lamppost? Or one of those plastered across the doors of houses? He could whack the boy hard for it. For maiming the bird, tearing the names.

"Garima Basu." How he wished he hadn't come along with Shruti. But the owner lifted his eyes from the poster. "Isn't that Srijan-babu's wife? The woman who does all that drama?"

"My aunt," Shruti said as she stepped out of the glass enclosure, happiness bold on her face.

A dead quiet fell over the place. Sonali nudged the girl next to her and whispered. They looked at him. Sharply, Ori looked away.

"It's a play by Jean Anouilh. About Joan of Arc," Shruti said crisply as she counted out the change to pay for the call. "You should go see it if you can." It unnerved Ori, the disdain sharp in her voice.

The owner broke out of his daze. "Yes, of course," he said, clearing his throat. "We're all so proud of her in this para."

The eyes were on Ori now, crumpled in the corner, trying to look small. Eyes like the blinding white of spotlights.

That's her son, that pale pretty boy. Nine or ten, maybe.

"Oh, yes," Shruti flashed a shiny white smile. "I know you are." Her eyes narrowed. "Out here, people just can't stop bragging about her."

✦

He stepped out, walked ahead as fast as he could. Faster, he urged himself. But no matter how fast he moved, he couldn't shake off the white glare of the spotlight around him. He knew that everybody on the streets stared at him.

"Slow down, nutcase," Shruti called out.

Garima Basu. The red and white letters screamed out at every passerby. He saw them turn around, stare at him as he broke into a run. Young men outside tea shops peeked at the writing on the wall, pointing at him, burning cigarettes stuck between their fingers. That boy, that one with thick glasses and pink lips. He heard shopkeepers bark at him, furious at the damage done to their shampoo and detergent ads. Sensing his fear, stray dogs licked the redness off the letters and trotted after him. Torn posters floated in the breeze and chased him as he ran.

He walked into the maze of crooked letters that ran circles around his home. Shruti's voice grew fainter behind him. Then he couldn't hear it anymore.

He walked into darkness. His heart beat faster, and for a moment, he longed for streets with light, shops, and people milling around in knots. But he walked on, slowly, his eyes gradually getting used to the dark. The walls closed on him and his right elbow brushed against a jutting brick, the slimy softness on it. *Moss.* The surfaces were thick with it, and banyan roots that wedged their way past the skeletal bricks, through the loosening mortar, walls bare of letters, posters, graffiti. Never. Ori paused. He no longer heard footsteps following him.

Wings flapped high above his head. Pigeons. Old pigeons that had forgotten how to fly. Through the window before him, he could see a room he knew well. He paused, then stepped into the house, pushing open the weather-beaten door marked for the sweeper, the only one to pass through it, twice a week.

5

Ahin Mullick walked past the cobwebbed shutters of the ticket counters of The Pantheon.

A red-hot hammer of anger throbbed inside his head.

The lobby wound around the circular auditorium all the way to the stairs that led upstairs where Ahin lived and tip-toed around all day. It was a price he had to pay for living above the most miraculous playhouse in Calcutta.

In a daze, he stepped into the lobby that darkened slowly as he walked toward the stairs. The grimy gloom of these passages felt unreal—even today. He still got gooseflesh, feeling the crowd around him, pressing in on him, their bony elbows jabbing him hard in the ribs. Fifteen years. Fifteen years had gone by since such a crowd had flooded The Pantheon.

The inner passage of the lobby was black as night. It had become the murky interior of a factory. Several tiny factories, with air thick with odours—glue and gunpowder and fresh paper, metal and machine oil. The Pantheon couldn't make a living anymore from being just a playhouse. Except for the Saturday plays with plump, belly-dancing sluts that drew in the horny truckers, performances were rare, just a couple of shows put on by local amateur groups. To make a little more money, the hallway had to be rented out to small businesses. Printers of wedding cards, firecracker makers, basket weavers.

He walked past a huge pile of paper and cardboard. Koyna was shuffling around the place where the printers were making covers of children's books. She was working with the sheets, folding them, playing with scissors and glue. She was alone. The men she worked with never arrived before noon.

Sharply something came alive in Ahin.

Not a week had gone by since that woman had bared her fangs and claws to wrench her son away from him. Thoughtlessly. The metallic twinge of pain from the incident still haunted him, left him with a sharp desire to beat the mother's body into pulp. Savagely she had dragged her son out over the threshold of the room. Brutally she had flung the shirt at the boy, the unbuttoned shirt that had clouded his pale body, hiding his perfect shoulder blades, his half-born, restless nipples.

Koyna looked up and saw Ahin. She smiled at him. Her white teeth shone in the gloomy yellow light.

For a moment, the hammer of anger stopped banging.

"Come here," Ahin called her slowly.

Koyna stood up. She was a cocky woman, not shy with men. The curves of her shapely body shivered as she swayed and laughed with the bare-chested men sweating over the piles of gunpowder and rusted iron machines. She liked men. She liked to touch them, fall over their bodies. Not shrink away when they ran a swift hand of caress along the back of her neck.

"Come with me," Ahin said now, turning and walking away.

The mother's fingers had left warm, red marks on the boy's bare skin, gleaming in the weak yellow light of the tiny room in Ruby Theatre.

Ahin walked down the winding flight of stairs. It was crammed with broken furniture and wicker and sackcloth and mangled billboards, seamless under a thick blanket of dust. Sure of touch, Ahin groped his way down.

Stepping into the basement, he flicked a set of switches on the wall. Powerful lights came on, making him blink. He heard clumsy, tentative footsteps behind him. Koyna was still feeling her way down the stairs.

Ahin looked ahead. The basement held a tidy home. There was a bed with soft, curvaceous pillows, over which a simple cotton bedspread had been drawn. Plastic flowering creepers, clean and dusted, were strung around the bedposts.

The heart of the basement was a massive iron pillar. It gleamed in the light.

On the other side of the pillar, a small wicker fence guarded a patch of plastic grass. Sprouting through the grass was the wooden figure of a tree with painted leaves. Lovingly it shaded a stall with a bunch of clay figurines. Just like in the Pujo carnivals.

Koyna, too, was sweet and kind. She stood at the landing of the stairs, a smile in her eyes. She would give him what he wanted.

"Lie on the bed," he barked.

"A thousand rupees," she said, coming closer, and opening up a palm upward.

"What?" Ahin paused.

"A thousand rupees," she repeated, the smile still soft on her face.

Ahin groped inside the pockets of his kurta. Clutching at a few notes, he thrust them at her.

Koyna sat down on the edge of the bed and unfurled her palm. The notes spilled over like a bunch of crumpled, dried flowers. She licked her finger and counted them quickly.

"Just 360 here." She smiled slyly.

Staring at her, Ahin realized why the workmen were always trying to touch her. She had finely etched features and a skin with a dark, angry glow.

He touched her face. She was real. Her skin was soft and rough at the same time. Soft on the surface, but very quickly beneath, it revealed a fiery toughness that drew him more powerfully. She was perfect.

She was Lila.

Her lips were a small, tender, blistered animal. She laughed as he ran his fingers across them. Entranced, he caressed her neck, pushed her down on the bed.

"A thousand rupees," she said again, looking up at him from the soft pillow.

Anger flashed like a purple streak in the dark. For a millisecond, his body tightened. Quickly he let it relax.

She had stretched out on the bed. A sleepy, smiling body. Her eyes were almost closed. Light glistened on her eyelids—a keen light. But her outstretched arms spoke the language of trust. They wished to melt into the softness of the bed. They were curved, slippery arms, shiny with sweat.

She belonged here. To this bed, to this set. To this play.

She was Lila, the lean and dark girl, the angel of affection. She was a key character, the soul sister of the lovely Meera, the heart of the story. Someday Meera would come too. *She had to.* But today, Lila was here. Lila of the melting smile and the rough-and-tumble skin. And pigeon-like breasts that promised to peck at your hands.

Trembling, he cupped them, squeezed softly. Her warm skin rose to his touch through her threadbare blouse. They were generous, kind, reassuring breasts. They could nurse and nurture and love.

But how would Lila sound when was ready to leave the life of the brothel?

He *had* to know.

"Repeat after me," he spoke sternly and slowly. "My pickle will tickle their taste buds just as my body fires up their loins."

Her face furrowed into an ugly frown.

"What nonsense you speak!" She raised herself on her elbows. "Where is the money?"

The world began to melt. In his nostrils, Ahin smelt the acrid odour of heat. Painfully he drew himself together.

"Repeat after me . . ." He repeated Lila's life-changing lines.

Roughly Koyna flung the sari anchal back across her body. "No wonder they call you mad. They should." She pushed him. "And a cheap one too."

Heroically he tried to put the world back together. He pushed Lila back down to the bed. Where she belonged. She would remain the whore. *Till she uttered the life-changing words.*

But claws sprouted through her dark and slippery body. Claws and hot, hissing breath. She lunged at him, a snarling animal.

He gave up. She would not learn her lines. She just would not.

The stage had started turning. Slow, and then fast. Like windswept candles, the lights flickered frantically.

Sharply he hit her face. Shrieking, she fell back on the soft pillow.

This was how the pimps held her down when she acted up. Act I, Scene 3. *Remember?*

Of the two pimps, Bullet had the most punishing fist. Heavy metal rings crested his thick fingers. Metal that cut through Lila's flesh. Again. And again.

Ahin knotted his knuckles hard. Ringless, they looked naked.

Faster, the stage swirled in his head as his balled fist hit the other side of her chin. Lila groaned, as if in mangled sleep.

There was nothing he could do anymore. He heard the prompter's angry cursing. Stubborn, stubborn Lila.

He dragged her body down from the bed. Across the floor. Softly she moaned again. She was a cursed sleep talker. A near-lifeless heap of flesh next to the shiny metal pillar.

Light and sound danced along the walls of the hall. Thunderstorms. Galloping armies. Hissing tidal waves.

He opened a glass box under the switchboard. The dusty glass hid a dark red lever. He pulled the lever down.

The giant pillar of metal stirred soundlessly. Harder. Ahin pulled down the lever harder.

The wooden sky above the pillar came off the hinges. Slowly it began to descend.

The magic stage.

Coming down, the wooden sky became a massive wooden stage. Slowly it came down like a dumb beast, slowly swallowing the shiny metal pillar.

The basement darkened. Suddenly a giant cloud had cast a shadow across the sky.

Something stirred Lila. The descending darkness. The heavy breath of wood. Slowly, surely, until it came down, the magic stage. Gently it would come to rest on the floor. Lila's half-words would be lost forever. There would just be a shiny pool of blood.

Lila shuddered and groaned. Life came back to her in the form of a sharp shriek. Like a wounded lizard, she slithered away from the lowering shadow of the giant wooden cloud above her.

She shot to the stairs and vanished in the dark pit.

Ahin looked at the vanishing figure. Tears swelled up in his eyes, like a hurt child.

6

Before going to bed, Ori combed and brushed his grandmother's hair. Every night. He loved to play with the gray-white strands. He would undo the neater braids woven by Maya earlier in the evening, comb out the sparse strands, make uneven, odd-shaped plaits. Suddenly his Mummum seemed small and weak and breathed the sad smell of an old woman in bed. The smell of coarse cotton and old wrinkled skin made his heart ache.

Sitting behind her, he couldn't see her face. For that he was glad, as the wrinkles on her face had a life of their own; they could speak a silent language that made people do as she wanted. He was scared of her face but loved her nightly voice.

As he braided her hair, she told him stories. Scottish romances carved in Bengali, found in the brittle pages of a massive tome in the library of a small town several hours from Calcutta by train. The terrifying origins of the *Arabian Nights*, stories spun by the fear of death, grown to life in a rich landowner's library in a village in Hoogly district, in a sprawling mansion where his grandmother was growing up, many, many, many years ago. Stories that needed no paper or libraries, stories that floated in the air through time. The gods and the demons churning the ocean for the nectar of immortality, the gods cheating the demons of their fair share.

She gave him endless stories, his Mummum. As she spoke, she taught him to possess the twists in the tales, the rhymes in the poems, even the moments of climax. She drew him into riveting worlds so that he could be a storyteller too, slowly, handing over to him the reins of the stories and the poems, bit by bit. By listening, he too became a teller, and there were many tales they told each other, one line at a time.

But sitting on her bed, slumped over a pillow with its stale old-woman smell, Ori sometimes wanted to cry. His mind kept running to his mother. She rarely came back before he fell asleep. He would see her in the morning, laying out his ironed clothes, preparing his school lunch. But for the night, he was left with stories in the soft voice of his grandmother, and fallen strands of white-gray hair.

She was ready with one of their favorites today.

"He was to board the ship," she said, "and set sail across the Arabian Sea."

It was the story of his grandfather's trip to England as a student. A story that never grew old. She spoke so often about the past that over the years he could see everything clearly. She spoke of his grandfather's whimsies, how he had appeared in the royal court of George the Fifth when he passed the barrister's exams, dressed up like a prince with a massive turban exactly as in the giant oil painting across Mummum's bed.

"When you've seen nothing but blue-green water for weeks, the stillness of the sea becomes scary. And the phosphorescent glow at nights! He couldn't bear to look out at the sea or to smell the salty wind, and for days he would curl up on his berth, in a tangle of blankets, getting sicker and sicker as the soiled smell of the bed seeped into him. 'I thought I would die,' he told me so many times."

Ori knew the lines by heart. Often he would give her a line as she groped for it. Sometimes, he knew, she deliberately missed a turn in the story so that he could draw her back on track; it pulled him deeper and deeper into the story, made him fall more deeply in love with it. *Yes, Bikash, that was his name, the other Bengali copassenger.* Loosening the hair from the tangle of Maya's braids, Ori felt a closeness to Mummum he could not imagine was possible between two people. He wanted to be the perfect boy. He wanted to braid her hair beautifully.

"He didn't even know how many days passed that way," Mummum went on. "Later Bikash would tell him that he had been sick for two weeks. Then the day came when he groped his way out of bed, his head still reeling, trying to walk around in the cabin, even stepping out on the deck. *I would sometimes go and sit near the rails, somehow keep my eyes open. I would inhale the salty air by the lungful. But slowly, I was getting better.*

"It was on those evenings that he saw Kartar."

"Mummum?" Ori said. "I'm making the braids with four plaits tonight." The four-plait braid was trickier than the standard braid with three plaits. You had to remember the order in which the parts had to be woven into one another, beginning all over again after you finished a single loop, carrying on till you came to the end of the strands of hair to create a pattern like the carved border of a silver bowl. He wanted to do something beautiful today with her wispy gray hair. He wanted to make her happy. Very happy.

"Yes, why don't you?" Mummum always let him do her hair any way he felt like. "And then slowly, he could never quite remember how exactly, he started talking to Kartar."

"Kartar was from Punjab," Mummum spoke slowly. "Your dadu said that his Hindi sounded more like Punjabi. 'Often,

I'd no idea what he was saying,' he would tell me. 'But it didn't take me long to realize that he was made to work alone because of the hatred sweeping over the ship.'"

The bed creaked with the weight of a human body. *Shruti.* Right next to him. She had slid into the room silently, bringing with her a familiar metallic perfume and the coarse smell of cigarettes.

Shruti did not smoke. The cigarette smell was of Filter Wills, Abir's brand. The smell sickened Ori. Why was she here? She stayed out of Mummum's way whenever she came home late.

He turned to Shruti and mouthed silently: *Where were you?* Shruti's face was flushed with happiness. *Cinema*—her lips formed a silent answer. She seemed kinder, softer than ever, nicer to Ori than she had ever been. *What movie*—he whispered, leaning closer to her, inhaling more deeply the coarse odour of Filter Wills. *Back to the Future*—she whispered back. They had gone without him. Had not even cared to tell him that they were going to a movie. Why? Not that he cared. *How was it*—he whispered.

The movie? I have no idea. Lazily, Shruti rolled her eyes and whispered, a careless laughter spilling through them.

Ori's fingers stiffened on Mummum's hair. He lifted his eyes to look at the ancient clock on the wall to the right, above the blue water filter. It was past ten o'clock and still his mother wasn't back.

"Putli," Mummum said coldly, using the baby name that Shruti hated. "How many times I've told you not to sit on my bed before changing out of your outdoor clothes? God only knows where you roam till late in the night and what kind of muck you bring home. Go wash up."

Shruti looked like she had been slapped. Ori thought she was going to say something bitter and nasty. But she curled her lips in disgust and left the room.

"You know what Kartar told your dadu?" Affection cradled Mummum's voice. *"They can kill us and throw our bodies overboard and everything will be hushed up.* They were the white seamen, full of venom for the black and brown men working on the ships, at the docks of London, Glasgow, Liverpool, Cardiff."

But Ori dreamt not of ships but the dark bowels of cinema halls. Where did they go? Where were they showing *Back to the Future*? He wanted to hug Mummum, bury his head in her neck along which green veins stood out like fault lines on an ancient rock. The grandfather clock struck ten thirty. His mother was still not home. He felt his eyes well up with tears.

There was a scraggly knot of boys from the senior classes in school who claimed to know all about the cinema halls in central Calcutta. About every movie they showed, even the booze they served in the attached pubs. Sometimes they would scurry into the darkness and sit behind the couples. *The stuff you see there is hotter than porn.* The movie on screen? You're funny. *They have no idea.*

The acrid smell of Filter Wills cigarettes clogged his brain. Abir's brand. Shruti never smoked. And nobody could smoke inside the hall. But Abir was always coated with the smell. How long was the movie? Was it just the two of them there? Did anybody else go with them? Did the scraggly knot of boys sit behind them, mesmerized? Nausea shot through his blood like an electric current.

"But dadu was still ill, wasn't he?" He tried hard to clear his voice. "He was terribly homesick now, right?"

"He missed them all," Mummum said tenderly. *"I just wanted to go back, get back to the firm soil of Calcutta. I missed my mother."*

The cluck, cluck, cluck of the lizard in the room echoed in Ori's brain.

"Mummum," he said, pausing on a breath, his fingers frozen still over a braid almost done.

"What is it, Ori?"

"Mummum," he repeated, fear and excitement battling within him. "Ma and Samiran Uncle were in bed. And they were kissing."

She swung around with such sharpness that he feared that wisps of her hair, locked in his fingers, would get wrenched from her scalp.

"Where did you see them?" Her face looked ashen. "*When?*"

He remembered the scene. It had been a slow and strange play. In that scene, they had ended their evening in bed. They came back together after a long day's work, entered the living room after a shower. She had rubbed her shoulder-length hair with a towel. Her homely nightgown had hugged her body like an old dress.

"They were in bed together, kissing," he repeated mechanically, staring at the mocking hands of the clock. "Where? Where?" Mummum's voice trembled and grew faint.

He would tell her everything. The story of his mother slipping into bed with a man, of their laughing quarrel under sweaty, crumpled sheets. With the meaningless noise they had poured into each other's mouths.

He'd seen it all on the stage. Easily he left that out.

Twice he'd watched the play, and many rehearsals of it. It showed a dull evening. Where the two stretched their limbs and cleared their tongues before an eager audience. Where they chatted through their dinner, fought over which radio channel to listen to.

"Ori!" His grandmother pleaded like a little girl. "Tell me where you saw this."

The couple looked more bored than tired when they got into bed together. The lights had dimmed but the audience could make out the silhouette of their bodies, entangled under a single sheet. Against soft background music, they had started reciting the list of the next day's groceries, their bodies fused together.

Actually they hadn't kissed at all.

But he had ached inside to see her weave another life and home, a life of daily grocery shopping and cooking and household chores. It had made him cry. It didn't make sense.

Half a kilo of small potatoes, remember. *Loudly, she'd insisted.* And onions of course, the red ones. The yellow onions are no good. And some spinach, and *potol.*

What kind of fish? *Rui* or *katla*?

The music rose to a crescendo. Their bodies drew closer. But for the two voices, it could have been one person sleeping on the bed. A large person who fidgeted impossibly.

"In Samiran Uncle's house," he said aloud. "That evening they fought over which radio channel to listen to. Later, they were in bed together, kissing."

Tears pooled around his glasses again, trickled down to his cheeks, and along with them rose within him the fine thread of anger that had flared against Shruti. It was as if someone had hit the old woman with a cricket bat, swung full force. *He only wanted to make her happy.* She was the only person who never forgot him.

"I was in the next room. Ma thought I was asleep."

But that was true. She never knew if he was there. She didn't care. Not when she was playing her part.

Not even if he was in the first row of the audience.

Never when she played her part.

7

Abir's bike zoomed ahead, edging its way through tiny cracks of space between stranded taxis and buses, past the hollow flanks of autorickshaws but never quite touching them. Sitting pillion behind him, Ori felt his heart would pop. Whizzing past the jagged edges of danger drew him closer to Abir, to a rocky, throbbing intimacy that made him sick.

"You okay?" Abir glanced sideways.

"Yes," Ori said. "Am I sitting right?" he asked, suddenly shamed by his own eager voice.

"Nice and tight," Abir shot back. "Better than your cousin. She scares a lot easier! Nothing like a scared girl with a hot body riding with you!"

Tremors shot through Ori. This was Shruti's place. Did she wrap her arms around Abir when they rode? He wanted to pull his arms away from Abir but the thought of letting go terrified him, dreading being tossed through the road, the giant wheels of buses crushing over his body.

Ori felt a jolt while Abir rode over a small pothole, chatting lightly all the while. Ori clung tighter as the bike wobbled on high speed, a sick feeling rising from his stomach as the coarse smell of Filter Wills cigarettes swirled in his brain.

He wanted to slap himself for agreeing to come with Abir. Why did Abir suddenly ask him? To go out with him and his friends for dinner? That too on a day when Shruti had to get back home early? He didn't do right. But the tangy dishes at Hakka restaurant were tempting, a distant memory from the days when his father took him places, the dim cave where the air was heavy with the fragrance of braised shrimps. Abir had looked at him with a curious glint in his eyes, asked him if he'd like to come along instead. "Why don't you?" Shruti had narrowed her eyes, as if daring him to go. But he knew her voice well—she'd be *really* happy if he did. Swiftly he had hopped on Abir's bike outside the college gate.

The gushing wind against his face infected him with the speed. Nothing mattered but this sensation of being lashed till the skin felt raw. It was as if Abir wanted to rip through everyone on the way, fly ahead with a trail of blood on his path—through old women gingerly boarding city buses, mow down the thatched walls of shanties fringing the road, smash the makeshift stalls with neat displays in rows of green coconut and cauliflower picked off the marshlands, scattering bamboo and wicker and vegetables like confetti as he went. With a sudden spurt of speed, Abir stunned a little boy in rags dithering over whether he should cross the street, the bike growling at him as it whizzed past, drowning his rickety frame in petrol fumes.

"You're flying!" Ori whispered as the bike burst out of a tangle of cars into a breath of open space. He twitched his nose nervously to balance his glasses.

"Fun, isn't it?" Abir looked sideways as he spoke, his words half-lost in the gale and the bike's roar.

Ori laughed weakly.

They left Saint Xavier's before dusk, riding north along Central Avenue. It took them almost an hour to reach Shyambazar.

Finally they were gliding into their para, its moist and slippery alleys now dark with the onset of evening. The bike stopped at a restaurant framed by a yellow and purple gate guarded by a spiky dragon. Chinese culture as nourished in north Calcutta.

The sharp smell of vinegar and soya sauce welcomed Ori and aroused a dreamlike memory. Back when he was little, he used to be terrified of the dimness of the lights inside the restaurants. The fragrance merely thickened into a knot and always mingled with his mother's perfume. But there was no flavor then. The food served on his plate had no taste. It was too dark. He could not taste what he could not see.

But today he felt comforted by the darkness. Abir led him to a table full of voices and faces from the winding lanes that contained his life, from the shops that lined them. They were all there. Trinankur, the local councilor from the municipal corporation, a muscled man in his forties with adolescent pimples, was nursing a frosted glass of Coca-Cola; beside him sat Pilot, one of his boys, who loitered around Trinankur's front porch all day. Beautifully crafted smoke rings danced out of the mouth of the small, middle-aged man to Pilot's left, the owner of the beauty parlor cum telephone booth from where Shruti liked to call Abir.

"This is where the para gathers in the evening." Abir pulled out a chair for Ori.

"Sit down, Oritro." Councilor Trinankur's smile was warm and slippery. "Would you like a Coca-Cola?"

Ori nodded. He would *love* a Coca-Cola.

Two men sat at the far end of the large table. One of them looked rather like Trinankur himself, a younger man who had his face and the same bushy hair. He was Trinankur's youngest brother, Dushtu, a keen member of the neighbourhood watch, people who kept the para peaceful. The other man was dark and middle-aged, with a leathery face and thin black-framed glasses. About him there were many stories.

Ori knew the stories. Everyone in the para did. The man's name was Tatai. He was a gangster who had given up a life of crime to run a roadside restaurant that now did good business. Mini Hotel. Its *biryani* and fire-hot mutton *chaap* were legend. Now Tatai was one of those men who watched over these lanes, kept them safe. Looking at him, a quiet and sullen man counting out change at the cash counter of his hotel, it was no longer easy to believe that he had killed people in the past. More men, they said, than he cared to remember. Teenagers cracked jokes about what kind of meat went into his tasteful *chaaps* and curries, jokes that annoyed adults smothered quickly.

"You know Dushtu, don't you?" Trinankur pointed at the man with glasses. "And this is Tatai-da." Hesitantly, he gestured toward the older man. "From the Party. They head the local citizens' council."

The Party he knew. *Who didn't?* Their office stood right next to the football grounds, under the bright painting of the hammer, sickle, and the star. The men played football all afternoon and then gathered in the room in the evening to paint banners for strikes and protest marches. Grim older men in shirts and pyjamas broke up fights on the football fields and brawls in the government ration shops. Everybody knew it was much easier to settle disputes at the Party office than at the local police station. They both belonged to the Party but the police were lazy and would not work without bribes. Things moved fast at the Party office and the cadres always helped people in trouble.

But Ori had never heard of the citizens' council. Who were they?

"What would you like to eat?" Abir placed a menu before him, a long sheet of laminated paper, smudged near the corners. A tall glass appeared before him, the fizz settling slowly on the dark pool of Coca-Cola in it. Through the blue haze of cigarette smoke dancing around the table, the glass looked like a dream. He hesitated.

"I want to go home." Suddenly he felt uneasy.

It made them unhappy. Anxiety clouded the table. "Why?" Abir reached out and held his hand. "Come on, I know you love Chinese."

"Relax, Oritro." Trinankur's voice caressed him. "What would you like to eat?" Across the dimness, the councilor's eyes were aimed at him, straight, kind, and soft.

"But," Ori said, "I have to go home. They will worry."

"Who will?" Abir asked, his brows dancing.

Ori fell silent, not knowing what to say.

"Let's order some starters," Trinankur said with a smile. "What would you like?"

It was kindness you could not spurn. Kindness that caressed him slowly. "Fried prawns!" he said.

"Good choice." The smoke-drowned owner of the beauty parlour spoke for the first time.

"And what else?" Abir asked.

More? Hesitantly, Ori looked through the menu. Szechwan noodles with gravy?

More food was ordered around the table, endless names ticked off on the menu. Dreamily, Ori stared at the picture at the top of the menu—a skinny old Chinese man with a thin, pointy beard in a chef's uniform, face split open in a cartoon grin, prancing along with a whole roast chicken balanced on a tray.

"Funny picture," he heard himself say, quite before he realized he had. Suddenly the sound of his own voice made him anxious; he stopped short.

"Oh, yeah." Abir leaned in to take a look and then drew back. An undercurrent of laughter trembled around the table.

"Do you still draw, Oritro?" Trinankur asked. There was a softness in his eyes, a softness brushed with a smile. It made Ori eager to talk, but all he could do was nod.

"I remember the Vishnu you painted in the children's sit-and-draw contest," Trinankur said, his eyes gazing off toward the swinging door to the kitchen, squeaking closed and open every other second. "Year before last, right? It was beautiful."

Ori looked up and stared at Trinankur.

"He had it down to the last detail." Trinankur looked around the table, a glow on his face. "The chakra, the lotus, everything. And he was probably just eight at the time."

Trinankur remembered it clearly. It created a warm feeling in Ori's chest.

"I remember it from the awards ceremony that year." It was as if Trinankur knew what Ori was thinking. "I was struck by the choice. And then the details. The details," he repeated.

A hand came to rest on Ori's shoulders. Softly. Abir's.

"Hey, you don't like Coca-Cola?" His voice was warm and soft. "You haven't touched it."

Ori sipped at the Coca-Cola. The sweet fizz simmered on his tongue and made him faintly nauseated.

Large plates of noodles and entrees arrived at the table. Golden balls of fried prawns, chicken, and capsicum in thick, fire-like sauce, cubes of what looked like boneless fish in heaps of sautéed onions and chillis, more plates of dense and dark sauce with tiny islands of food sticking their heads out. As the waiters started ladling out the food on the large china plates laid out before them, a fractured chorus went around the table, directing the fried prawns on Ori's plate. And a good helping of Szechwan noodles. And some chilli chicken. And that he should eat more.

Undecided, Ori took another sip at his Coca-Cola. It did taste bitter, with a bizarre twist to it, sharpened by the swirling cigarette smoke all around him.

"Try the fish too." Abir ladled a large portion into his plate. "It's panfried." He used the serving spoon to make space on Ori's plate, separating the noodles and the prawns in neat, distinct zones with a tenderness that suddenly saddened Ori for reasons he couldn't grasp.

"Why did you choose to draw a picture of Vishnu?" Trinankur asked in a voice touched with wonder.

"I like to copy things," Ori said. "I copied it from my mind."

"Where did you see it?"

"My Mummum has a framed photo of Vishnu in her prayer room. She prays before it every evening. It's a really nice picture."

"His grandmother," Abir said, pushing the tall glass of Coca-Cola closer to Ori.

The fried prawn had made Ori thirsty. He took a long swig at the Coca-Cola. The nauseating fizz went down his throat like a flood of cold vomit. His head swam, as if he were afloat in air.

"Your Mummum is your favourite person in the house, isn't she?" Trinankur asked, his voice soft.

Ori nodded quietly. It was not something he could describe. His Mummum was the source of everything that was reassuring and real. But he liked to hide this from the world. He couldn't imagine a life without Mummum and yet he was desperate to grow out of this sticky, shameful need.

Trinankur was silent now, but his eyes remained locked with Ori's, in a kind of a pact that excluded the others at the table. There was safety in Trinankur's company, in his gentle smile. Ori looked down again, at the crescent of prawns across his plate.

"You tell her everything, don't you?" It was strange listening to Dushtu's voice. It kept growing fainter. It seemed to come from far away.

"So tell us," he leaned ahead. "When did you first see your mother with Samiran Uncle?"

Terror clutched his heart like a black, sharp-clawed bat, killing his desire for sweet and sour fish. An acid wave of vomit rose to his throat. All eyes were on him now, even those that pretended to look away.

Trinankur just sat there. He chewed his food furiously. His pimples jumped up and down as his jaws moved.

"We know you've seen them at his house," Tatai's voice crawled toward him, like a buried animal slowly coming back to life. "Doing things to each other."

"Oritro?" The voice cut through the darkness. "*How many times* have you seen your mother with Samiran?"

His mother?

The woman who'd fought with vultures? Over her brother's grave? The one who'd been Antigone, out in the windy nakedness of the Maidan grounds under the dark evening sky? The stubborn, hotheaded woman who pierced through her clothing of shyness to silently fight everybody around her?

He wanted to eat. The fragrance of fried prawns had merely sharpened his appetite. He tried to ladle some sauce with his spoon, stab at a piece of meat with his fork. But his hands, weak blobs of jelly, couldn't make sense of the darkness on his plate. It was frustrating, and strangely it made him want to laugh. The laughter weighed down on him, wrestling him to the ground, pinning his arms at the elbows till the fork clattered against the rim of his plate and bounced onto the table.

"You're not doing this right." Trinankur's voice came from the wilderness. "I was getting to it gently. He's a child, remember?"

"Yes, I saw that," a voice whirled. "Going on and on about paintings. Then it would be school, and if he likes Mughlai food better than Chinese. And then, cricket. Smooth!"

"You need patience for some things. I didn't win the elections three times running being a brute."

"Who do you think you're doing a favor?" It was moving, the intense energy in Tatai's voice. Quickly he turned to Ori again. "Does your mother go to this man's home often? Do they meet elsewhere?"

"There's no one else in the graveyard." Ori heard his own voice come from a distance. "Just the vultures."

"What?" Dushtu looked like he had been punched in the face.

The cutting had been from the leading Bengali daily. You had to squint to read the caption beneath the picture. *Garima Basu in the role of Antigone. Produced by Max Mueller Bhavan.*

"The vultures were live." The words circled around his head, again and again, before he could utter them. "And the Germans taught her to jump across the trenches. She had her brother's dead body across her shoulders."

Trinankur reached across the table, held Ori's hand. He leaned in closer. Electrified, he pulled back. His pimples swelled like red dots on his cheeks as anger flushed his face.

"Did you give him booze?" He looked around the table, ready to kill.

Abir moved the glass of Coca-Cola away from Ori. But not fast enough for Trinankur, who snatched it away, the dark liquid sloshing around inside. He sniffed at it, thumped it down hard on the table.

"This is rum laced with Coke," Trinankur thundered. "Whose idea was it?"

"Was supposed to be Coke laced with rum," Abir said. "I guess someone got carried away."

"The vultures were perched on the wall across the graveyard," Ori said. "Not stuffed birds. Live ones."

They didn't seem to care anymore.

"This was a mistake," Trinankur said, despair in his voice. "The whole thing."

"Get real, Dada," Dushtu said. "The citizens' council has sorted out a lot of messed-up families, and sometimes you need to twist the knife a bit. Nothing the Party doesn't know already."

"This is a family we care about. They've lived here for generations," Trinankur's voice boomed. "This is not some drunken rickshawallah who beats up his woman in the slums every day. You can't just throw a kid like this in a pool of rum and get the scoop out of him."

Right next to Trinankur, Tatai roused himself from a sleepy darkness. When had he taken Abir's place? And why was Abir nowhere to be seen?

A clammy hand wound around Ori's back, rested heavily on his right shoulder. "You saw them in bed? How . . . er . . . you remember what they had on?" Stubby fingers slipped past the collar of Ori's T-shirt and rubbed his skin gently, ever so gently, to the rhythm of the question, repeated in a whisper. "Or did they?"

He was a smooth man. His hand a blob of kindness on Ori's skin, he looked across the table to Trinankur. "Do you realize how serious a problem this is for us? At least five families have come up and told us that with their own daughters growing up here, this woman is a shame to have around in the para. She spends all her evenings in the theatre halls in dirty neighbourhoods and comes home way past midnight. Rupa-Boudi came to my house last Friday and told me that the woman sleeps with other men right in front of the boy. He told his grandmother everything just the previous night!

"In the end, it is the Party who has to watch out for the people," the grating voice shot through the air again. "I told Rupa-Boudi, don't say a word. We'll find out what happened. And then we'll fix her."

The first bout of vomit rocked him from within before spurting out of his mouth. Stunned, Tatai recoiled. Watery, with tiny islands of food floating in them, the vomit streamed into the fire-red gravy of the sweet and sour fish, flooding the boatlike bowl in which it had been served, spilling on the table. The second wave shot spasms through his small body, his head dropping down into the bowl of sweet and sour fish, sweet and sour vomit.

Tatai's right arm wrapped around him again, this time clutching his ribs. It was a deep hug that squeezed more vomit out of his quaking frame, the acid burning his nose. "Should have gone easy on the booze," he said, softly massaging the shaking body. "Need to take him home now."

Chairs screeched against the floor as they were pushed back. The foggy outlines of bodies rose together; more hands hugged him and helped him to his feet. His hair was now soaked with sweat. He felt the dampness settle into his skull.

―※―

He flopped down on the rough softness of the backseat of the taxi. His back, sticky with sweat, had caved in. He tried looking out of the window. Everything was slippery and changeable, semireal through a glass jar of stirred water. Street lights, knots of laughing people, shops with their shutters down. Women leaning out of balconies. Rickshaws resting aslant at street corners.

Voices cluttered his head. Memory of hairy fingers with thick rings and a burning cigarette held between them.

They knew everything. The Party. They circled around their lives. But Ori had never meant them to know anything.

It was just a story. Mummum was not supposed to tell anyone. He never told her stories to anyone.

But Mummum had told his story to others.

Coughing, he asked the driver to stop. "But," the man protested, "they've asked me to drop you at the blind lane. And they've already paid me."

"It's closer from here." His voice sounded like it belonged to someone else.

He stepped out, angry with himself at the way his legs failed to hold his weight. He hated the driver's arm around his shoulders, steadying him. He tried to adjust his glasses with his finger but they were moist with vomit and slithered on his skin. Beneath his feet, the ground was now softer. The walls closed upon him, and his right elbow brushed along a jutting brick, covered by the slimy softness of moss.

Suddenly wings flapped high above and settled back into silence. Old pigeons that struggled to fly.

He stared through the window in front, at a room he knew well. And then he stumbled into the house, pushing open the weather-beaten door marked for the sweeper.

8

He woke up the next morning to the sky turning pale over his head. The early morning light showed a strange world. He realized he was lying on a camp bed on the terrace of their house. His head hurt. Why was he here? Had he come up here on his own? Questions awoke in him like slow cramps. Did someone bring him here? *Did he sleep here all night?*

His mother sat on the edge of the bed. Quietly she stared at the sky. Sensing him awake, she looked at him.

A fine shiver went through Ori's body as their eyes met. But his mouth was dry; the flesh inside felt metallic, coated with rust.

Slowly she started talking, her eyes wandering away. Her voice had no warmth, a voice that refused to touch him. It kept a sharp distance.

"Where were you last night?"

His heart thudded in his chest. Stale vomit nudged the back of his throat.

"With some friends," he said slowly. "With older boys from school."

She turned to him. Her face darkened. "Were you out with Shruti's friends?"

"No . . . No. Just some boys from school."

"Did Shruti know about this?"

"No!" His voice trembled. "It was . . . there was . . . just those older boys from school."

She looked at him. Her eyes looked strange. Had she been crying?

Slowly, he felt his voice gain strength. "Boys from Class Nine and Ten." He spoke slowly. "They were fooling around with drinks."

He paused, looked away. "They gave me some . . . and . . ."

She breathed quickly. Through the corner of his eye, he saw the rise and fall of her chest.

"I don't remember anything else," he said sharply.

A thread of anger seared his veins but vanished suddenly. Everything was dark and disheveled and there was no fresh air to breathe at all. Not even on the open terrace where he had perhaps spent the night. *Perhaps.* He couldn't remember what he did last night after getting home. Nothing whatsoever after hitting the threshold of the dark, untouchable door at the back of the house. What had he done? *What?*

And then suddenly there was a giant hole where his heart had been. The story returned. The story he had whispered to Mummum while braiding her hair. Now it belonged to the Party. The Party which ruled these narrow alleys and the chipped walls and the balled fists of millions of angry men painted on them in red.

She would never know—the tall and pale woman who sat on the edge of his bed.

"If you could see yourself last night," she whispered to him. "If you could hear your own voice."

He felt a surge of terror. What had he said? What had he told her? *What?*

"How would you ever know?" Did she feel the fear shooting through his body? "What it is to see a ten-year-old in the state you were in last night? Your own ten-year-old?"

Her very own. Slowly he breathed again.

"Promise me that you will stay away from those boys in school. I know how it goes. I know it better than I ever wanted to." She looked into his eyes.

She looked like a little girl when she said that, and it shot an arrow through his heart.

><

The house staged a miracle: it hid that night from Mummum. Nobody could bear to imagine what might happen if the old woman got to know about it; no one *dared* to imagine. That her ten-year-old grandson had got into bad company at school and come home drunk, sick, and smeared with vomit. Anxiously the maidservants swabbed the floors and spread lies quickly to keep the house clean of stench. The boy had gone out with his mother and come back with her, long after everyone had gone to bed. It was an innocent story, sown in the air by Rupa, mouthed by the maidservants like a mantra. They were all terrified of the seventy-year-old widow in fragrant white.

Later in the day, Shruti came around and spoke to him in a low, hot whisper; she simmered with the anger she had to hide.

"What the fuck happened last night? Where did you guys go?"

"Hakka," he whispered back.

"Who was there?" Her eyes had narrowed.

"Trinankur." Fear clutched his throat as he said the name.

"Trinankur? From the Party?" She grimaced, as if at a bad odour. "What the hell was *he* doing there?"

"I don't know. I don't know." Suddenly his whisper was like a shriek. *Leave me alone.* "They were all drinking so I wanted to drink too. Coke." He turned and hid his face in the pillow.

"Good for you!" She looked at him in disgust. "And who asked you to make up this crazy story? Older boys from school getting booze and passing it around?" Sharply she looked behind. There was nobody in the room.

A shimmer of anger exploded inside his head.

"Like you care! All you think about is having fun with Abir at the cinema." He stopped short, shocked by the smell of his own mind.

He looked up. He saw that he had nothing to fear. Shruti's face had lost its colour.

Abir's crooked smile flashed before his eyes. *Shruti didn't know.* Not the story he had whispered to Mummum. Nothing of what had happened last evening. Nothing at all. They had managed to fool her. They all had. How did they? Shruti could pin you down and wrench the truth out of you. And smack you hard for lying. *Bloody hard!* But Abir had fooled her. And how he had fooled her too.

The house had to stay sane. It could not sway. They all pretended nothing had happened, and quickly smoothed out the rough edges under Rupa's sharp guidance. The maids followed Rupa's script to perfection. They whispered among themselves. But they protected the rest of the family from that night's incident, swiftly and affectionately. Rupa made sure no news of the incident reached Ori's father—the easiest thing to do, for he paid less and less attention to everything these days, rarely speaking to the neighbours or even to those at home. Locked up in their bedroom during most of his spare time, he sometimes watched cricket on their small TV set. He slept a lot.

Rupa nursed Ori relentlessly, directing the maids to squeeze fresh fruits for juice and make a simple fish stew for his lunch. She did not speak to Ori's mother, but worked on Ori tenderly. She did not look shocked at all. Ori could not have made it through the day without her care. But her composure created a sinking feeling in him. It was as if she knew this would happen, one day.

But the ground had cracked and shifted under his mother's feet. Nobody had cared to protect her from that night. Shock had steeled her at the break of day. But it became clear soon that the terror she stirred in Ori that morning was more of his own early morning panic than anything else. She was nothing to be scared of, really. She did not lash out at him in any way. She had no strength. She was nothing to worry about. As panic shattered her, she only tried to cling to him, hugged him so tight that it hurt.

She skipped her rehearsals for the next few evenings. She did not want to let him out of her sight for a second. She rummaged through his school books, the rucksack he carried to school, checked the buttons of his school uniform to find out if any of them needed sewing back on. She planned to take him to the eye doctor; he had myopia and needed checkups at least once a year. She would ask him about his friends every day. Who did he sit next to in class? What games did they play at lunch break? What kind of food did his friends bring for lunch? Who came to pick them up after school?

But she could not find her way around his life anymore. He had shot up too fast. Everything about him was long and bony and stupidly angular—his knees and the spines of his new books in school and the frames of his new glasses. She was trying to grope through a world that had slipped away long ago. He was thin, too thin. Years and years had gone since she had mashed boiled vegetables into his rice with a dollop of ghee and had fed him while he read a book.

He had grown strange new needs that puzzled her, like help with homework that became more and more difficult, exams that grew more complex and elaborate, a new kind of shoe for PE classes, haircuts that had to follow school rules. Everything that Rupa had taken care of quietly all these years, so quietly that nobody had noticed it at all.

But his mother tried. Tried to make sure he never went out of her sight. Winter came around in a few months and she got an invitation to travel with her theatre group to a small suburban town, a few hours from Calcutta by train. Ori recognized the town; it was close to his aunt's house in Hoogly. She had to go, his mother told him. And this time, she was going to take him along on the trip. Suddenly he felt excited.

There was a time when this would create a fight in the house. People would raise their brows and roll their eyes around; he would face a grim-jawed grandmother, a stray cruelty from a loving neighbour. *Go join the circus. You'll return a monkey with furry paws.* Our child? Perched on the hard seats of green local trains speeding through the stench of cured leather and rotting fish, while hundreds squatted beside the tracks for a fresh morning shit, headed for some village shack without electricity or filtered water? They'd never been to these places, but they knew. And with whom would he go? Rowdies of the theatre, drunken, loose-limbed louts? That halfwit Pallabi, who clung to Garima's hair like a crushed comb?

When Rupa heard about Garima's plan to take her son with him on her stage tour, her jaws tightened; she said nothing to question her sister-in-law's decision but suddenly became cruel to the maids. Quickly she killed their whispers and hushed giggles and drove them hard to finish the day's work.

Ori's mother had made up her mind. She packed a bag for Ori—neatly folded shorts to wear indoors, a white kurta to wear outside, notebooks for homework, Charles and Mary Lamb's *Tales from Shakespeare* from English class, the worn rubber flip-flops he used at home. She did not even forget the bitter red ayurvedic toothpaste he hated to use.

She didn't care to tell his father anything. It didn't look like he cared to know. The rules were changing.

9

Mani Mullick had left his older brother, Ahin, with a terrible burden. *The Pantheon.* The most miraculous playhouse in Calcutta.

Mani was Mani, the little mad boy who had poured all he had into the black hole of the theatre. And why not? Theatre was sacred, had always been so in the Mullick family. They had owned Indralok Theatre on Beadon Street since the days of the British. Other landlords had their suburban garden houses and their singing Lucknow courtesans. The Mullicks had their own playhouse—all through the crazy years leading to the Partition and beyond, till the family lost its land and orchards to clan-squabble and the playhouse had to be sold off to the Kajarias. Bleeding Marwari traders, buying up the theatre para! What did they understand of theatre?

Mani went berserk when the family lost Indralok. He was like a bloody widow whose husband had been killed in the Indo-China war. That was the year of the war. Bloody nuisance. Mani couldn't care less; all he wanted was his own theatre. A playhouse he'd seen in Soviet Russia had blown his mind. The auditorium, with its seats and aisles, revolved around the circular stage, taking the audience on a trip around the play, in between scenes. He blew his share of the family estates to chase the dream and came up with something crazier, a revolving circular stage at the heart of a circular auditorium that remained stationary. The Pantheon. The stage would sink to a pit below in between scenes, float up out of it loaded with characters in the story who were to play out the next scene. Had the world known anything like it? Circular walls enclosing the auditorium where lights zoomed and splashed and sound echoed, horses galloped and tornadoes moaned and sound technicians slapped at mosquitoes inside glass cubicles? Had the world seen anything like it, ever?

The Pantheon was built right inside their ancestral mansion in north Calcutta. It stood proud in the heart of Calcutta's theatre district that ran from Shyambazar to Hatibagan. The stretch between Cornwallis Street and Upper Circular Road thronged with playhouses where Calcutta's rich and the sleek went to play. You just had to look at the long line of cars outside the halls, the Buicks, the Jaguars, the Fords, and the Austin Morrises. Silken days they were! The best novelists wrote stories for the theatre and the priciest cabaret singers from Firpos and Trincas sang and romped on stage. Mani, the crazy kid, he had jumped into the carnival like a trapeze artist and dazzled them all! He'd had the colossal hallway on the ground floor of the mansion remodeled into a lobby that wrapped itself around a ticket counter bursting at the seams.

But lightning ripped through the sunny sky. Mani kicked the bucket at the tender age of forty-eight. The fried batter of his favorite mutton cutlets went straight to his heart and clogged the valves, the doctors would say. The bastard never listened.

He committed suicide, that's what he did. He didn't want to live any longer. The rot, he knew, was going to set soon. After one hundred years of light and cheer, Hatibagan came apart like a spent carnival, all torn tents and dead lights.

The lifeline of The Pantheon was clogged as badly as Mani's arteries. Ahin refused to sell the playhouse, but as people's love ebbed around the theatre district, the lights slowly started going out in the auditorium. Slowly cobwebs replaced the crowd of playgoers waiting in snakelike lines that wound all the way down to Upper Circular Road. The excitement died, and the odd play or Independence Day and Republic Day gatherings, complete with song and speech, failed to draw a soul who cared about theatre. A pestilence struck the city.

There was a reason why Mani had left The Pantheon to Ahin. Ahin would never sell it to the Marwari theatre wallahs. *Never.* He lived in the cavern of the house, the only creature there, in the floor right above the auditorium; he brushed his teeth and peed and pooped and tiptoed back and forth above the greatest stage in the world. The stage had remained in the family—left to the care of the elder brother too lazy to die, too deeply burdened with the blood share of genius.

For six years now, Ahin had let himself bleed, a little bit at a time, to write a play for the magic stage. *Dusk* was now ready but unborn, a sketch in ink craving the colours and animation of life. Six characters out there mingled in the air and dust of the streets, lingering in homes that offered half a peek into their interiors through windows, bodies that belonged to his play but had not found their way to it. One by one, the years went by. Elusive faces and voices teased Ahin, in parks and crowded buses and fish markets, never giving in to his yearning.

He had to go out and seek bodies that he could touch, bring home, bodies that he could crush and caress at will. Bodies that would melt.

For *Dusk*, the play in three acts, waiting to rise out of the dark pit at the heart of the most stunning playhouse in Calcutta.

10

The sprawling stone turrets of the temple spread out against the sky like the petals of a lotus. It did not look like a temple but a palace that had weathered hundreds and hundreds of years. There was none of the damp, shrieking chaos that made up real temples; the stone and burnt clay spires held the silence of ruins.

Ori had only heard about this temple from Mummum. It was a bit of a myth, etched and carved by her stories. Hundreds of years ago, a raja had built this temple with stone and burnt clay. Hidden inside the delicate sculpture were shrines of Kali and Shiva. It was the place for which this little town was known.

Ori walked in the direction of the reddish brown turrets. He walked toward them quickly. He had slipped out of the little house where the troupe had put up, without anybody watching him leave: the men smoking and toying with the wigs, the backstage players, the hairdressers and the makeup folks and the set boys shooting back and forth past the balcony. Even Pallabi, who always watched him out of the corner of her eyes, had not noticed: the show was about to be staged and she had her nose buried in his mother's hair, working breathlessly, blind to the world.

   He ached to go back home. His mother had brought him to a poor and cramped world. A trip on a crowded local train and a house where the men had to pee in the open and a lumpy bed crawling with bugs. His mother couldn't go to the bathroom since they had arrived as there was only one bathroom with a real door and there were too many people crowded around it. Discomfort had tightened her features, strained her smile; it made him angry and ashamed. It always happened whenever he traveled with her troupe. He could never understand how she could change her clothes in a room full of other women who laughed and whispered and smoked cigarettes that smelt foul.

   Stepping out, he had thought of walking to the station and taking the train back to Calcutta. Would anybody miss him if he just went back? But he didn't have the money to buy a ticket.

   Like a fairy tale, the cluster of stone turrets had suddenly warmed his heart. The dingy, smoke-filled house of theatre was gone from memory. The temple evoked old ruins, one of those shrines where nobody prayed, where people just strolled amid greenery surrounded by an earthy kind of cleanliness. But the place was not ravaged. The delicate filigree of burnt clay grew alive and beautiful as he walked closer to the shrine walls.

   There were only a few people around, lost in the sprawl of sculpture around the shrine and the trees around the courtyard. Dust hung in the air, a kind of dust which had a certain scent, the blend of wood, stone, and clay. Walking across the courtyard, he saw two beggar girls moving between the scattering of tourists, wheedling kindness out of them. The younger girl, he realized, was blind, and was being helped around by her companion. They seemed part of the temple, along with the red earth that stretched before the shrine and the white balustrade that surrounded the wide courtyard.

He slowed down a little to watch them. They were both young, but the blind girl's companion was older, perhaps eighteen or twenty, a slender woman in a dusty sari worn in the way that hinted at a life spent on the streets. Hesitantly they moved toward a middle-aged man wandering around the courtyard. The woman held the blind girl by the hand. The girl was smaller and younger, perhaps thirteen or fourteen.

Voices floated to him across the breeze.

"Babu," the blind girl murmured, groping her way toward the man. "I'm from a good family, but this is where fate has brought me. I was born in this town but have only heard about this temple." Her voice dropped. "I hear it's beautiful."

Ori paused a few feet from a tree and watched them from its shade. He felt strangely drawn by the girl's voice and the delicate smallness of her face. It was the kind of face that could distract a passerby, make him stumble a little. She reached out and touched the man's chin, caressed his neatly shaved cheeks, his lips coarsened with age, her hand sliding down, along his neck, dipping into his shirtfront. "Hey!" The man protested, but his voice sounded weak.

Sliding behind the tree, Ori felt safe and invisible.

"She was born blind, the cursed little thing," the older girl sighed. "She likes to touch people when she talks to them."

"What can I do?" the man protested weakly, cornered between the sprawling tree and the stump of an ancient pillar. "I'm just here to see the temple."

The blind girl's face touched the man's chest. She took a deep breath, as if she were trying to inhale the man's smell. She lifted her face and lowered her voice, her words stumbling against each other. "I wait every day to see the face of Ma

Kali in the shrine out there. She speaks to me in my dreams." She pushed the man farther back, into a warm crevice on the trunk of the banyan tree; her arm glided around his waist like a smooth snake. "I need your kindness."

"The operation will cost six lakh rupees, Babu," came her companion's voice from close behind, the tone clearer, crisper.

The sightless eyes of the blind girl fluttered furiously. She curled herself around the man's rigid body, the perspiring shirt drawn over the bulge of his stomach, the expensive watch which she scratched with her nails like it was a callus on her own skin. Softly her hand moved away from the watch, slid down his waist to his thigh. Her fingers dug into the fabric of his trousers, as if they were seeking something.

"What *are* you doing?" the man asked, breathing feebly. He glanced around quickly; his voice weakened. "There are people around." Beads of sweat had appeared on his forehead.

"She is such a happy girl, this little sister of mine," said the older girl, in a soft and moist voice. "Young and healthy, she'll play for hours and looking at her, you wouldn't know that she was born under such an evil star."

The younger girl reminded Ori of a puppet pulled by strings. A puppet with hollows for eyes. She grasped the man's right hand, brought it to rest on her chest. Limp at first, the man's hand slowly woke to life on the girl's chest, fingers spreading out across the top of the printed cotton frock.

Suddenly he drew back his hand as though it had touched a live wire. He pulled out his wallet, and a large rupee note from it. "Here, you keep this." He looked at the older girl. "I hope the operation goes well."

The older girl, as though in a stupor, took the note slowly from the man's fingers. "The goddess Kali will bless you, Babu," she said. "You are a good man."

Pulled by her invisible string, the puppet girl drew away from the man. Her hand lingered below his waist and gently caressed his groin before it drew back. Her eyelids fluttered again. "God will be good to you, Babu."

The girl turned to her right, a puppet blowing in the wind. Her closed eyelids faced Ori, leaning against the tree just a few feet away. It was muddling, like a beast's cold breath on the back of Ori's neck, the sight of the blind girl flashing a sharp smile at him. Forgetting, he stared back, then quickly turned his face away.

The man had stepped away. As he walked past Ori, he ran his palm over his shirt, stretched it over his bulging middle, smoothed the fabric of his trousers below the waist.

Ori felt drawn to the girls. But he walked away, toward the clean heart of the temple, the smooth marble courtyard that encircled the shrine. He didn't want to look at the blind girl again, lock eyes with the fluttering eyelids, imagine that he'd seen her smile.

As he walked away, he heard her voice behind him. "Babu, I've grown up here and have never seen this temple with my own eyes."

He couldn't help but turn back and look. The two girls stood in the way of three young men, picnicking types from the city, their clothes out of place in the earth-scented air. Intrigued, they had paused.

"Young and happy she is, this sister of mine," Ori heard the older girl's voice. "But the nerves in her eyes are all dried up."

Ori felt restless. He walked away as fast as he could.

The temple was empty, except for a few loitering tourists, and some stray dogs curled up outside the shrine. He walked up to the arch over the entrance to the shrine and stood there. The darkness inside made the shrine look like a giant toothless mouth. For a while, he stood there, drawn and repelled at the same time. He walked around the shrine, across the narrow, blistered terrace that encircled it. Behind, the burnt clay surface of the terrace had merged into a jungle of weed. The wild bushes looked fresh and young next to the ancient filigree on the temple wall. He sat down on the ledge of the terrace, his legs dangling just above the cool and moist undergrowth.

"Hey, kid!" a rough voice called out.

It was the blind girl. She sat at the other end of the terrace. *Hey, kid!*

She looked at him again, her eyes alive under lids that no longer fluttered aimlessly. She winked at him, and whistled again. "Hey, kid!"

She was leaning against her older companion, who sat with her back against the red and blistered wall of the shrine with her sari-wrapped legs dangling over the edge of the terrace.

"Come on over here," she called him.

Ori wanted to turn back, slide along the terrace, around the shrine, past the red-gummed mouth.

"Where's your mum?" the girl asked.

"Getting ready," he said hesitantly, "for her play."

"Play?" She frowned. "What play? Where are you from?"

"Calcutta." He marveled at her callused fingers, the thick rinds of dirt under her nails.

"Fuck the whoreson." She sat up and rubbed her left breast in exasperation. "My nipple still hurts, he tweaked it so hard!"

"The old guy, Didi?" asked the older girl.

"Didi?" He stared in shock, looking from one to the other and back.

"She's younger than me." said Didi. The elder sister, with dirt under her nails, gestured toward her companion. "By four years. Just tall as a pole so you can't tell."

Absently she rubbed her sore nipple.

"Not the old guy," she grimaced. "He wet his pants when I touched him. The fat driver in the morning. Pockets dry too, I told you he'd be a waste of time. Slipped his hand through the top of my frock, the bastard!"

Tall as a pole, her companion? Hardly. But she could say that, she who looked not more than a couple of years older than he was. So she was a midget. But what about that child-like face? The reed thin arms and the eyelids that fluttered madly whenever she was blind?

"You look much younger than her," he said haltingly.

"I look better blind too." She looked at him sharply. "Mithu would yellow her sari if she tried to drain their pockets."

"He was watching us, the little creep," she said as she glanced at Mithu, "when I was milking the old guy. Chicken!" She spat at the shock of green hairweed behind the shrine. "Pulled out a fifty as soon as I squeezed his dick."

Dreamily he came closer and sat down next to them. Revolted and fearful, he couldn't take his eyes off this girl. Was she really older than Shruti? Twenty? Older? She was barely two inches taller than he was. Those arms belonged to a younger girl. A child in every way but in her voice, a voice all spit and foul odour.

Didi. Big sis. Mithu called her Didi. But Mithu would poop in her sari if she ever tried to lick the men dry of cash, caress their bodies like her little big sis did to see them with lash-fluttering, dead eyes.

They might have pulled out dark, powdery stuff from the folds of their saris and frocks, perhaps cheap cigarettes or tobacco hand-rolled in dried leaves, but they toyed only with the weed under their feet. Mithu chewed on a blade of grass, her eyes glazed, and her Didi caressed herself with another uprooted tuft. The setting sun shone on the bare skin of her neck above her frock.

Ori wondered why they let him linger, talked nice to him. What did they care?

"My mother's friends are putting up a play this evening on the big field," he said, looking around quickly before speaking.

"Must be the high school football grounds." Didi exchanged a glance with Mithu.

"Everything happens there," Mithu said. "Carnivals, plays, and the big Kartik Pujo. Even the big gatherings before the elections."

"But it's just the locals, none of the city folks go there." Didi chewed a twig and blew air through her teeth. "We keep away. Bloody *haramis*, the local boys. They just paw at our boobs but never give us any cash, the whoresons."

"But they'll throw cash at your mama when she dances there tonight, the haramis like the pricey city chicks." She spat out the piece of bark she had chewed off.

The words felt like a slap on his cheek. Heat flushed his brain. "She doesn't dance. It's a play."

"A play," Mithu yawned. "Dull blather."

They hissed words that rushed blood to Ori's cheeks and made his heart beat faster. But it was easy to slip into that dark and moist world. They slithered through the tall grass and flung stones at the dogs that dozed behind the shrine. Mithu squished slimy worms with her bare big toe and beheaded them with her overgrown toenails. Didi whistled sharply. Mithu turned around and they were gone in a flash. A man had stepped out of a car in front of the temple courtyard. Quickly the girls came back, Mithu biting her nails and Didi cursing her sharply. "Whoreson came with his wife and she's a bloody hawk, shrieks at anyone stepping close to her husband." Quickly they forgot about it and flung stones at squirrels shooting across the tree trunks, which seemed to laugh at them before vanishing in the leaves.

The hours flew by and the sun went down behind the burnt red shrine. Didi stood on the terrace, stretching her reed-thin arms above her head, the hem of her long frock rising like a soiled curtain. The sun sank behind the forest of weeds and Didi swirled her tongue around, flinging words at Mithu, words nasty and nice, at the dull-green forest, the grazing calf lost there, the barking temple dogs.

The colour of the sky gave him panic. "It's late," he said. "What if they all leave for the play? How will I get there on my own?"

Spitting the blades of grass from their mouths, the girls laughed at him.

"You're not going to get lost, kid!" They laughed. "We know this town inside out."

※

Out there on the grassy football grounds, she was no longer his mother. She was a girl-woman who had left her teens through the rite of marriage, the iron and white shell bangles of wedlock around her wrists. As Ori made his way toward the makeshift stage set up on the far end of the field, his eyes were riveted to the red light cast over the bed of the dying peasant who was being tended over by his new granddaughter-in-law.

The play was etched in Ori's mind. *The Enchanted Garden*. There was a lovely garden owned by an aging peasant, coveted by the zamindar of the village. The zamindar lies in wait for the peasant to die so that he can seize the property and grab the garden for himself. But the peasant grows more robust with age as he pushes past ninety, nearing one hundred, till the zamindar dies instead, his lust unsatisfied. Greed dies a hard death, passes on to the new zamindar, the dead man's son, who lurks like a vulture, waiting for the old peasant to die. But the peasant grows healthier, nourished to senile beauty by a new granddaughter-in-law, till the health of the new zamindar begins to wane, prematurely, weighed down by desire that had haunted generations.

"My mother," Ori murmured, his eyes glued to the red glow of the spotlight. The three of them were huddled together on the ground far from the stage, he and Didi and Mithu, chilled to the bone in the cold air without a blanket. *My mother.* He had pointed out, as if the figure in red had been standing right in front and could come over to them with a smile.

The story was timeless. He'd forgotten how many times he had seen it performed. In an ancient theatre in central Calcutta, in a high school auditorium in Bhubaneshwar organized by a club of expatriate Bengalis. He always knew what would come next. Love would kick out death. The caddish grandson, the only blood relation of the aging peasant, would lure a young woman, the lissome Padma, into marriage, bring her home to his ancient grandfather bitterly guarding his blooming garden.

His mother played Padma even though Padma was younger than she was.

On the ground, the crowd breathed heavily.

On stage, Padma, the sharp-tongued woman with a heart of gold, sat at the old man's deathbed. She bloomed like the flowers in the garden. Her warmth spread to the old man's deathbed and spilled colour on the soiled sheets, the grainy texture of his skin. She gave him warm glasses of milk and the breezy air of handheld fans. Distant on stage, she was less defined, younger, and her prickly youth, sharp words, shrill voice and all, passed into the old heap of the dying man, till a perky spark of life wriggled through his bent spine.

Her hair was slim, sharp in its blackness, the angry tail of a mare chained by a wildflower, brushed into glistening, sweaty perfection by Pallabi.

Soon the grandson shot out on the stage, euphoric at the news of his wife's blushing pregnancy. Fruits mellowed in the old man's garden, stooping close to the ground.

"I have to go pee." Ori rose, his body a crooked letter on the grassy ground. Hesitantly he looked at Didi and Mithu. It was dark and cold out in the field, and he didn't want to go out there alone.

"You hold our place, Mithu," Didi said and got up. "I'll go with the kid."

The dry odour of burnt tobacco floated toward them as they made their way past the field of blanketed bodies, dark and covered like corpses scattered on the ground.

The bodies thinned out as they moved farther and farther away from the stage. It was as if they were walking toward a cavity, a giant crater fringing a plateau on which the people sat, huddled around the dancing fire of the stage.

"Over there," Didi said as she pointed her finger toward a thick growth of shrubs. "That's where the men water the plants."

The dank smell of urine guided them toward the shrubbed blackness. Like dogs, men liked to urinate against something, a wild knot of grass or a bush, never on naked flat ground.

He went and stood as close to the shrubs as possible. Hesitantly he looked over his shoulder at the small woman a few feet behind him, her small frame nebulous in the dark.

"Oh, I'm not looking," Didi said sourly. "Not dying to see another dick right now!"

A hot flush gripped his head and spread over his ears. Not daring to look back, he unzipped his pants, taking out his penis, its veins bursting with the need for release, grateful for the shadow of his own body that shielded it from the small woman behind him, small enough to pass as a fourteen-year-old. Bared, his skin felt naked in the cool air, and the sound of simmering urine against the bushes slowly filled him with warm shame, like blood rising in his cheeks. He wondered if the woman standing right behind him could see the glassy arc of piss shining through the dark.

But she had wandered, a little farther away; the rustle on the grass revealed the movement of her small feet. The stage was a tiny halo of light, far away in the darkness.

Tucking his limp penis back inside, Ori zipped his pants, the stench of stale urine suddenly hitting him with wild force. He stepped back.

"Done?" The small figure floated toward him. "Let's go back."

They walked back, but the flickering light of the stage muddled their steps. They wandered a little, and as they drew closer to the stage, they found themselves far from the place where Mithu was keeping their places warm for them.

The stage seemed to have crept upon them unexpectedly. They could see the laughing, shrieking bodies on it through the hollow shell of the wings, a tiny passage created by sticking bamboo poles through a stretch of canvas, where characters vanished offstage for a few seconds before treading down the wooden steps. The two of them crept close, and then closer still, blinded by the angry flickers of light and the deepening human voices on the raised platform.

Gupi, Padma's husband, had just found out that his wife would give birth after another seven months; his soul thrummed with joy. Standing close to the stretched canvas, Ori heard the thump of Gupi's callused heels on the hollow wood of the makeshift stage, leaping from one end of the stage to another.

An old man with wobbly limbs climbed up the stairs to the wings. It was the shrill, tortured ghost of the dead zamindar. His doddery steps shook the wings. The naked flame of the lantern danced madly.

Didi whispered, "Padma is going to hatch her egg, her tummy's bloated like a bull's hump."

For a millisecond, Ori dreamt of smashing a fist into Didi's face, watching her writhe on the ground. But the dream melted in the cool darkness of the evening as he stood still next to the wings. He looked up to the narrow passage to the stage above the wooden steps. His eyes paused at the lantern with the naked flame, a salivating tongue of light tamed by a fragment of cloth wound around the mesh of wicker sticks where the lantern was perched. The coarse sheet was tied behind the lantern in a way that it served as a screen, keeping the gusts of wind from the tiny tunnellike passage along which the characters stepped into the story.

Didi whistled. "They've stuffed a pillow under her petticoat, look at the way she waddles!"

They had lit the passage carelessly. The tongue of flame flickered as if it was about to lick the canvas sheet. Ori stared at it, as if under a spell. What happened to the glass dome that usually protected the lantern's flame? The tongue swirled inside his head, licking the flesh of his brain, making him wince.

"Didi," he whispered. "Look at the way they have set the lantern. If the wind gets to it the flame will set the canvas on fire."

"Yeah," Didi said. "The idiots, they don't care."

"If someone just would pull that cloth away."

The stage lights and the flicker of the lantern flame had tinged Didi's face with a red glow. Her smooth face glistened with sweat.

"Wood and cloth," she whispered, her voice trailing away. "It'd be like a firecracker."

Breathing sharply, he climbed up the stairs. Didi followed him. They were like two dark insects, barely visible. The lantern was perched higher up than either of them could reach.

"I'll lift you up," Didi said, quickly bunching her arms around his light frame. Revolted, he was struck by the strength of her arms. She aimed him like a spear in the direction of the flame, which came closer to his face, blinding him. He tugged at the rectangular canvas wrapped around the mesh of wicker and realized quickly that it was tied more securely than it looked. The golden tongue slithered inside his head while he worked at the lantern, his thighs trapped between Didi's strong arms and the warmth of her chest. In a few seconds, the cloth hung loose. Madly, the flame danced around.

Terrified that it might go out, he flung the end of the unhinged cloth over the flame. Immediately the flame spilled over. The cloth meandered like a snake in the heat and scalded his face. Didi's grip loosened and he slid to the ground, their footfall drowned by the loud voices on the stage.

They scurried down the wooden steps to the damp grass below. He followed Didi, who knew better than to run behind the stage, into the emptiness where they would stand out as suspicious, antlike figures. Instead she slithered into the disheveled crowd of people close to the stage.

On the stage, life struggled on, the greedy landlord now in a fit of rage provoked by the new life about to bloom in the house where he wished death to visit. As violence broke out among the characters, the left wing lit up, a sudden drunken burst of light in the narrow passage just beyond the stage.

Ripples went through the sea of people before the stage. Bodies stirred and rose, bones creaked out of cold, lassitude, and blankets. A wicker fell to the left of the stage, a floating arrow in flames.

Fat tongues of fire licked their way out of the wings and froze the landlord's anger into stunned silence. They pulled out people not meant to be on stage, bewildered, directionless, and unleashed shrieks that were not meant to be heard in the play.

Ori stood on the road, far from the stage. Dreamily he looked at the flames. They were no longer just inside his head. Not anymore.

11

*D*usk. Ahin called the play *Dusk* because everything happened there as evening rolled around. As the sky swiftly changed colour and the air thickened with the nasal cries of flower sellers—just beyond the windows through which Meera and Lila stared at the world. On the browned pages of the notebook, the story was disembodied, half-real, mere lines. Ahin had given birth to it, and yet it was not fully born. For that it needed flesh and blood. Bodies he could seek and caress at will.

Meera and Lila. Two women who made their living pleasing men, giving them a home for a couple of hours in the evening, mixing their drinks, pouring out honeyed words. Warming their beds. Lila the dark one, Meera the fair beauty. Soul sisters to each other.

But *Dusk* was Meera's story. It was about the curve of her smile, her soft laughter, the weakness of her flesh and spirit. About her hunger for a home and a hearth, the carelessness with which she flung it all away. About her lovely hair, noosed around her neck after death.

He would create a little boy for Meera. A beautiful boy with smooth lips and a shock of shiny black hair. To be sent away to play whenever his mother had a lover. A boy who never had to be told when to leave the room. He knew it from the fragrance in the air, sprayed like light rain, the new sheets on the bed, the sudden blooming of languor in his mother's limbs.

One evening, there came a man who was different.

Mrinmoy was a guilt-ridden newcomer unable to lift his eyes off his own feet as he cautiously sat on the far corner of Meera's bed. He could not bring himself to look at the woman whose evening he had just bought, not daring to inhale the fragrant air of the room. Meera's little boy liked this man, this man boyish in his hesitation who would smile only at him. *Not* at his mother.

Just as the boy was about to leave the room, Mrinmoy, the hardy trucker blushing like a child, reached out and held his wrist.

"A sweet boy. Yours?"

"Yes," Meera said, amused at the courage he had gathered up to talk to her. "Mine."

"Where's he going to go in this dark?" He looked up, pleading. "Let him stay."

"*Let him stay?*" Meera rolled her eyes, her brows dancing.

"Oh . . . well." Mrinmoy's hand fell away from the boy's wrist, a piece of dead flesh. The perversity of his own words struck him like a bolt of thunder. His ears reddened.

Laughing, the boy fled the room.

But Mrinmoy was doomed to be more than a part-time lover. He was fated to go beyond the pleasure given for the notes soiled with sweat and engine oil. Beyond the sweat and fragrance he got for his money. He never quite lost his hesitation, his guilty love for Meera's son whom he never again tried to hold back while the boy's mother unveiled her body to him. But *Dusk* had its own life, Ahin's perverse pen did.

Soon Meera and Mrinmoy grew to clutch each other with a need not granted to prostitute and patron.

Mrinmoy gave her marriage, a home. Meera left the brothel, kindling in Lila the hope of a cleaner life and livelihood through the charm of her homemade pickles.

Intermission. Lights to come back to the hall. Soda and popcorn to bring back relief as the magic stage sank slowly back into the pit under the auditorium.

The magic stage would rise again with Meera and Mrinmoy's new house. It carried a soft bed with quilts hand-sewn by the mistress of the house and a little shrine of gods and goddesses in the corner. But soon the stage light would be split into two. The home pushed back to a corner, a carnival pitched itself across the rest of the stage. The field was dolled up; there were the merry-go-rounds and the juggler's tent, the snack vendors and the puppeteers, the happy couple wandering through the *mela* like two excited children. Quickly Mrinmoy got lost in the maze, keen to find something to delight his wife. The long shadow of a tall man appeared next to Meera, left alone at a stall; nimbly, he picked up her handkerchief that had dropped to the ground. Slowly he turned.

The shadow lengthened behind Meera. A man from her past. An old client who tenderly demanded her new whereabouts.

Shocked, she looked away, pretending she wasn't the one he wanted. But he clutched onto her handkerchief, drinking in its fragrance, the fragrance that had made up his evenings, now a thing of the past.

Just tell me where you live now.

It is me, Meera. But I've left the business. I have a home and a husband. Don't bother me again.

He held out the handkerchief. Won't she take it back?

Just tell me where you live now, my love.

Why, why did she do it? How could she, the captive, horrified audience would ask, the salt of popcorn still on their lips, clutching the arms of their seats. Why did she breathe out the details of her new home before turning away in horror, ashen-faced before Mrinmoy who walked into the spotlight just then, the terracotta earrings proud and gleaming in his hands. "I could not resist these! Just put them on, will you?"

She wiped the tears from her eyes and smiled at him.

The lights were pale yellow again, silhouetting the tall figure of the man who now came calling at dusk every day, when Mrinmoy was gone on his long, truck-driving trips and her son was out playing.

Like a deer blinded by the searchlight, Meera gave in every time. Every evening, just before her little boy rushed in from the playground, all sweaty and spent, the man left.

They played beautiful music the day Mrinmoy found the packet of expensive cigarettes in their bedroom.

Haltingly, Meera admitted to an occasional craving for tobacco. Mrinmoy listened with a smile, and kissed her fears away.

How deep was his love for Meera? The story would tell.

12

The autorickshaw created a rumbling music as it raced through the countryside.

Hoogly town. Where he wanted to go. Where he needed to. He had told Mithu and Didi, his words breaking up, as the three of them scattered from the destroyed carnival of the theatre. Cold water had been splashed on the fire, on the play, blankets had been pulled up from the ground, shouts and curses flung in the air. *No, he didn't need to go back to the house where the theatre troupe was staying. He needed to go to a house in Hoogly town. His aunt's house. Was that far from here? Far, but not that far. He knew it was the next station by train. Or the one after that?*

If he could find an autorickshaw.

Hoogly town, Pipulpati, the fire brigade house—that was all he could tell the autorickshaw driver. That was all he needed to know, the scruffy old man at the wheel told him, he'd been driving in these parts forever. Since I was your age, boy, and you sit right there. But it's going to be thirty rupees, okay?

Mithu and Didi slid away in the graying dark of the late evening. The engine gasped into life. Ori heard the noise but felt nothing. He could not stop shaking. He had a fever. He knew he did. But his skin was cold like a dead animal's. He huddled in the back of the auto. He closed his eyes. The flames came close to burning him but his skin was still cold, like he had already died.

"Jesu everywhere," the scruffy old driver chattered. "They filled up the riverbank with churches, the Dutch and the Portuguese. You should see the lights now that Christmas is coming!"

The ribbed plastic curtain danced against Ori's face as the vehicle chugged past ponds layered with thick meshes of water hyacinths. He saw the curtain touch his face but he felt nothing. Nothing at all.

He lost track of time, his eyes closed. A woman with jingling iron and shell bangles floated through licking flames across a dark, grassy field. She bent down to caress him, but where was he? He woke up with the crackling heat of fire on his cheeks but found nothing but cold air streaming through the ribbed curtains of the autorickshaw. He shivered hard, ached for the autorickshaw to shoot faster and farther, deeper into the country.

"Fire brigade." The auto came to a pause before a massive, arched gate, the driver sputtering and coughing with his machine. Ori had fallen asleep; he opened his eyes to the expanse of the gated grounds, the fire trucks sitting on the grass like tiny, rust-dented houses, in the dark, a soothing sight.

"You can go in," Ori murmured.

Farting its way past the pond where they had lost innumerable cricket balls, the auto came to a stop near the main entrance of the house.

A short, dark figure limped out through the door. Shankar, the server-in-chief, commonly called Tea. A club-footed man who moved in and out of Ori's child-mind as the maker, bearer, and server of tea, morning, afternoon, and night, his dhoti and kurta inseparable from the smoky fragrance of Darjeeling brew his aunt loved.

Tea hobbled on his good foot, a thin flashlight in his hand.

"Ori *khoka babu*?" Peering into the auto, he shone the light at Ori. "You have come alone?"

13

It was a strange, large-hearted house. A fallen castle that had rented its grounds to the local fire brigade. Men in khaki shorts played football on the grass in the afternoons and often kicked the ball straight to the pond where it floated, a curious flower amidst the water hyacinths. Inside they lived in a cluster of high-ceilinged rooms that ran a ring around a sunlit courtyard. They played cards and spread out washed clothes to dry along stretched coir ropes, crinkled khaki shirts, and white vests browned with time. His widowed aunt lived upstairs.

He lost the entire month of his school vacation in that house. It was that kind of a place. Time slipped into its cracks and vanished quickly.

He wanted to forget. He could become a good person again. But the flames still hovered and licked him lovingly. He fought them in his sleep. The flames wanted to love him, but he clawed and scratched, tried to push them away.

Late that night, his aunt called up his home. To let them know that Ori has landed up here, the crazy boy, and all is well, and yes, maybe he can stay here for a few days. His Mummum's stern voice, he knew, would soften when she heard her daughter on the other end of the phone. But he was shaken when he picked up the phone. Anxiety and disgust fought each other in the old woman's voice. Home was beginning to crack and vanish, a world where once upon a time, the old woman could pull the entire family close around her fist. The house was slipping away out of her hands. Home, she said, was so poisonous for the young boy these days that he might as well stay at his aunt's place and smell the clean air.

His aunt's house entranced Ori. He spent his days in the musty air of closed rooms, with antique furniture that hadn't known the touch of human bodies in half a century, large, shuttered windows that were thrown open only for a few hours a week to keep the walls from crumbling into dust. His aunt was one of his father's elder sisters who had married into this family of lazy, happy landlords whose lands and orchards spread all over Hoogly and Chuchura. Nobody lived in the other wing of the mansion, the "brown wing." Carpets the colour of bloodclot stained dark floors. It hugged you in its underground warmth the moment you stepped through the door that linked it to the white wing, where his aunt lived. The "white wing," because of the expanse of marble all around. Sunlight bounced off the veined surface of the marble, dripped and flew in all directions, and poured in from huge windows that looked over the vast grounds surrounded by palm trees. *I've seen the brown wing lie behind heavy padlocks ever since I came in here as a bride thirty-two years ago*, his widowed aunt would say, the words hushing into silence. But it was a family without people. The small family had lost lives early; quickly they became smiling, garlanded photographs on the walls. All that was left in the massive crater of the house was the smiling widow, the elaborate ceremonies of her prayer, and the family of slow and wrinkled servants downstairs.

The sound of human feet was rare in that house. But it was full of breezy open spaces that were made just for vacations.

Its dreary birdsong helped cool the memory of the licking flames while he walked through the massive, high-ceilinged rooms, imagining Shruti's fluid voice echoing against the walls just like in holidays of past years.

One evening, Rupa came to see him.

She'd left work early to get here, make a three-hour journey—bus and train and then rickshaw from the Hoogly railway station. Her familiar pale-yellow sari and sweat-stained blouse suddenly took him back home. Rupa never wore the usual white cotton but did her duty wearing the same dull colours every day. Ori came out in an old pair of sleeping pyjamas that were too big for him, with flowers sewn around the wrists, and stood at the door, his mouth suddenly dry. He wanted to slip away but felt he couldn't drag his feet.

Rupa looked at him and laughed out loud. "Come here," she said. Slowly he walked up to her. She rolled up his sleeves in neat folds.

From the staff library at her bank, she'd gotten two detective novels for him. Byomkesh Bokshi, the lazy, sharp-witted, genius sleuth. Unexpectedly, it gave him a flutter of happiness. He had forgotten how addicted he used to be to these stories even a few months ago.

But she did not talk much to him after that, nor touch him again, not even to muss his hair. She spoke to Ori's aunt in a low, anxious voice, and quickly, they sent him outdoors to play. By the time he came back inside, Rupa was gone. His aunt's face had darkened; suddenly she looked tired. "You are going to stay here till your school starts again," she said. "Good thing you ran away."

He had never seen such darkness on her face. Questions raged in his heart like birds caught in a storm. But he did not have the strength to ask. When his aunt asked if he wanted to talk to anyone at home on the phone, he sharply nodded a no. There was no one with whom he felt like talking. Nobody would give him any answer. Maybe . . . maybe Shruti? But not now. He couldn't imagine facing her hard, probing questions.

The empty silence of the house sucked him back like the gentle pull of the earth. The tedium of birdsong and the rustle of leaves promised safety from human voices. He spent the rest of his winter vacation there in a kind of numbness that strangely grew pleasurable; the marble caverns of the mansion drew in his time wordlessly.

Around Christmas, Bandel church became a garland of lights dotting the river like a lit-up riverboat. On the day before Christmas, Shruti phoned in the afternoon and his aunt called him to the telephone. As he picked up the heavy, marble-topped receiver, he realized his palm had grown damp with sweat.

"What are you, crazy? Running away like that!"

His heart beat wildly. There was a sharp edge in her voice. Ever since that morning when he had mocked her about Abir, a grating unease sat between them.

She called again a few days later. And then again. *Why wasn't he coming home?* She was impatient.

"Seriously, Ori," her voice fell to a whisper. "You haven't called home even once all these days. Don't you feel like talking to us at all?"

Nobody at home, she said, had bothered to share Ori's whereabouts with his mother till she had left her troupe and returned home the next afternoon, shivering like a leaf in a storm, stage makeup still daubed at her temples. Everybody had looked away; nobody would speak to her. Shruti had slipped into her room and told her everything. How Ori, the crazy idiot, had run away from the troupe and landed in his Pishi's fire-brigade home in Hoogly. "It was as if I had slapped her." Shruti's voice fell. "She just sat quietly, staring in the blank. She didn't even want to come to the phone, talk to you."

Ori listened to Shruti's fast-paced voice, the sharp intake of breath. The questions returned and raged the old storm in his heart. But they never rose to his lips. Shruti hung up but called again after two days. And then she kept calling. When was Ori going to come back home? *When?*

Once in a while she would push away her uncertainty and try to bully him like old times. But it was a child's voice, a sulky child full of fear. It didn't scratch him. He said nothing about coming back home. Mummum took her turn to speak with Ori every time Shruti called. Her voice breathed a strange relief, as if she was pleased that he had run away. Was Pishi fattening him up with her chicken in white sauce? And the milk there, he must remember to have a glassful each in the morning and the evening, thick and creamy it was, nothing like the watery mix they sold in the city.

Finally, his mother called one day. But she said little, and nothing about that night. Her silence made him restless.

"You don't know how to swim," she said gently. "Stay careful around the village ponds and tanks."

"Yes," he mumbled, his heart twisting in slow pain.

"And don't forget the Odomos before you go to sleep. Arms and neck and shoulders. There are a lot of mosquitoes there."

Suddenly his throat choked; he was afraid to talk.

"You have to come back home by next Friday," she said. "School reopens on Monday."

Over the next few days, she sent him his clothes and a few more books along with the servants who traveled down the local train from Calcutta, along with two packets of his favorite vanilla-cream biscuits that were only available in the city stores.

Desperately he clung to the days of his winter vacation, days he could spend away from home. Time slipped by unnoticed, through the white marble crevices. The year turned.

When his thoughts looked homeward, he found himself thinking of Rupa, her smile that was, oddly, half a frown. He kept thinking of the way she had made fun of him, how easily she had rolled up his sleeves.

14

He came back home just in time for school.

It was the beginning of Class Six. New books, and there was going to be a new classroom on Monday, a new class teacher, the curly haired Miss Miranda who cracked equations with the same smoothness with which she played the piano in music class.

Same old school uniform with the white shorts, still another year before they could wear trousers.

White terry-cotton shirts like headless torsos flattened on the ironing board. Clothes his mother pressed always, all by herself, the steam hissing off the angry tail of the iron as she carefully edged it past. The green tie with gold stripes across it. The spiky steel of the silver badge pinned on the shirt.

She talked as she ironed the clothes. Her low voice pummeled his heart.

"I was relieved to see the stage catch fire."

She did not look at him. She looked down. Why wouldn't she look at him?

"A fire kills a play fast."

The white shirt emerged from under the iron, neat and square. Ori wondered how hot the iron was, about to come down on the white shorts, the seams along its loins.

"Why were you relieved?" His voice was steady but his temples throbbed hard.

"I just couldn't get up on stage that evening." She looked up. "I begged to be left out. Anuradha could do my part, I told them, with a good prompter. There was no way that I was going up there . . .

"I was done with the hair and the makeup when Pallabi told me that they couldn't see you anywhere. Her voice fell to a hush; she tried to hide something but it was right there.

"I heard everything. They were talking about the steep banks of the river and the railway tracks that ran naked past the town. Places to which the village had lost little boys and girls in ugly accidents. They fell silent the moment I came close, but I heard everything.

"And the stretch of the river past the town was deep." She looked into his eyes. "I never trusted your habit of wandering off places. I never will."

"I," he murmured—"I just went to the Durga temple. They said it was beautiful!"

"The producer came at six thirty and held my hands." She put down the iron and stared at him. "'Garima, we have taken 8,000 rupees from the local organizers—the whole amount, plus the cost of the trip. I just want you to come with me and look past the wings, across the field—just once. They're saying there are more than 700 people out there, come all the way from Chuchura, Srirampore, Chandannagore. Many of them have thrown money together to get us here, and so many of them have made a long trek to watch this performance. If we cannot stage this play tonight, there will be bloodshed.'

"Right then I wished that I could do something to myself." Her voice faltered. "Hurt myself so bad that they couldn't push me out on stage.

"I just couldn't pull my hands away from the producer's grip. *It's up to you,* he said. *I'm leaving with a bunch of local boys right now to look for Ori. We'll take the town apart if necessary. Your boy is the smartest out there. Nothing can happen to him.*"

On the dull white cloth of the ironing board, the flat-bellied steel frog let out a steamy fart. Ori couldn't take his eyes off it. Soon the crisp fragrance of burnt fabric would season the air.

"Ma, I was close by. I just went to see the temple. Mummum told me so much about it . . ." He bit his lips hard, stopped himself in midsentence.

"When I saw the smoke coming out of the wings, I realized I didn't have to go through with the play anymore," she said.

Quickly she came around from behind the ironing board, took him in her arms. "Were you scared when you saw the fire?"

"I . . . I couldn't understand . . . what was happening out there." He looked into her eyes, his body weightless in her arms.

"How far were you from the stage?"

"Far. Near the trees at the back."

"All alone!" She let him go, her palms resting on the bony ridges of his shoulders, circling the back of his neck.

"They had gone mad. They could have crushed you."

"Did someone hurt you?"

He felt her bangles bite into his flesh. Serrated gold leaving teethmarks on cold skin.

"No. They told me what happened."

"*Run, kid,* they said. *The stage has caught fire.*"

"How did you know where to go?"

"I ran the way everybody was going."

"Why didn't you look for me? You could see me on stage, couldn't you?"

Yes, he could. Yes, he could.

"I was scared." Slowly, he looked up at her, tiny gold bangle-teeth biting down on his flesh, harder. "I was running away from the stage." Away from you all.

She pulled him into her arms and crushed his face to her breasts. In her chest, on her neck, on the edge of her chin, there was a smell that never left her. There was the smell of clean cotton, sweat, light beads of it, a breeze of fragrance from her hair, and something else.

"I ran straight for the auto and asked the driver to take me to Pipulpati. The fire-brigade house."

"Told him that my aunt will pay the fare."

It was her very own scent—the faded, glue-like aroma of makeup remover, the smell which said *mother*. Remover that couldn't be removed. It stayed forever, throughout the night and the next day.

Her kisses nibbled at his face. Kisses wet with fear.

"Never slip out of my sight again. Stay right in front. Always.

"So that I can see you from the stage."

You.

Him. Only him.

On Monday morning, sixty sets of ironed white shirts and shorts sat quietly behind their desks. A gift for Miss Miranda. The new class teacher. Her skin like porcelain and curly hair like a doll's.

Miss Miranda was the reward of reaching Class Six. A reward, not a gift. *They* were the gift. Miss Miranda could pull apart the invisible strings that tied her gift, crackle open paper you couldn't see, and still have sixty pairs of eyes stare at her in wonder and a little fear. No one chewed gum. There were no stubs of chalk or paper pellets in flight across the class, not one appeal for permission to visit the toilet, a palm over the bursting soo-soo, dancing a jaunty jig. You just didn't grab your soo-soo in front of Miss Miranda. Out of the question.

Rich Yang, the tall Chinese boy who whistled through the window at women passing through the streets outside, was so quiet that he looked like a seated corpse.

Altaf Rizvi, the boy with the sad, pinched face, looked sadder than ever.

Shouvik looked the same as always. Seated upright, elbows always away from the desk, the owner of a healthy spine. Always. Once a giant lizard had fallen on his desk, along with a large slice of plaster from the ceiling. Shouvik had moved half an inch to his left and continued with his equations.

Shouvik was Ori's best friend. During lunch break, they always fought on the same side. Fought with their empty lunch boxes, sometimes with a half-eaten boiled egg plopping around inside. Tall and quiet, Shouvik was deadly at lunchtime; his steel lunch box knocked every other box off the fight.

Ori wished he were sitting farther away from Shouvik today, five rows behind him. At the other end of the room. He didn't feel like talking to him.

Outside, the day yawned and stretched upward through the fog in the winter air. While it did so, Miss Miranda went around the room and asked everyone how they had spent their Christmas vacations.

"Tell us what you did for the holidays. For Christmas and New Year."

Knitting her brows, she asked: "Before we start, does anyone need to go to the toilet?"

No one did.

She started off with the left corner of the last row, where the Catholic boys hung together in a tough knot. Matt Flannery had spent his holidays with cousins in Toronto and had seen ice sculptures. Christmas trees of pointy glass that would melt away with warmth rising in the air.

"Very nice," Miss Miranda said, as if Matt had just spelled a difficult word correctly.

Vinit Rathore had gone to visit his Dada and Dadi in Udaipur. Lots of marble sculpture there. And none melted after winter was over.

The class buzzed with laughter.

Miss Miranda smiled and said that was okay, certain things were seasonal, like mangoes in the summer.

Rich Yang had remained in the city. In their house overlooking his dad's carpentry shop a few hundred yards outside the school gates. Whistling at fat old Chinese ladies in loose floral pyjamas all day from his window. Ori was quite sure about that.

He had also attended midnight's Mass at Saint Paul's Cathedral. That was all he talked about.

"Oh, yes, it's beautiful," Miss Miranda said. "I was there too!"

Shouvik, too, had stayed at home in their house in Shyambazar, a ten-minute walk from Ori's own. The crooked lanes leading out of their house touched Shouvik's too.

Ori wished Miss Miranda would skip over Shouvik. Who cared if his aunt's family had come to visit from Bhopal?

Ori? He had spent his holidays at his aunt's house in Hoogly. In a huge, empty house built 200 years ago.

"Two hundred?" Miss Miranda knitted her brows again.

Yes, Miss. Fire trucks now lived in the stable once occupied by carriage horses.

And he had visited the Portuguese church in Bandel to see the Christmas lights across the river.

With his parents, of course?

"Yes, Miss." His voice fell to a whisper. "They came over for a few days."

"Very nice, Oritro," Miss Miranda said. Her smile began at the corner of her lips and then spread across her face, a slow sunshine.

He was the only student she knew by name.

She already knew him from arithmetic period in Class Five. A good student. Obedient. He had never been asked to step out during assembly.

And then the day woke up.

Late in the afternoon, the air became still again. The lull was finally shattered by the last shrill call of the day, from the bell high up on the wall. Parents gathered outside drew closer, like an expectant crowd outside a cinema hall where the next show was about to begin.

The door sentry opened the gate to let in the parents. And the drivers authorized to pick up children. The mothers followed, eager but anxious to trail at a little distance behind the drivers. Ori knew his father would take awhile to get there. His office was a few blocks away, right across the main street, farther toward Dalhousie Square. Too close to be punctual. Not that he was a man who believed in punctuality. At the office, he was the life of the party. He had too much to laugh about and too many cigarettes to smoke before climbing down the stairs and crossing the street to collect his son. With a large smile and a crazy plan. To have a late lunch of tandoori roti and fire-hot mutton *chaap* at one of the trucker's dhaabas that lined Bowbazaar Street, biting raw onions in between mouthfuls and hearing the tummy grumble. Or head on his motorbike over to Globe or Lighthouse to catch the latest release from Hollywood. With him anything was possible. Or so it had been once upon a time. Even the lingering mothers seemed to think so, swaying to laughter at his crackling humor, touching their hair often.

❦

The moment he saw Trinankur walk through the school gates, Ori tasted vomit in his mouth. Vomit that reeked of Coca-Cola.

He had seen Trinankur several times since that evening at the restaurant—a few times at their house, talking softly with his father and aunt, once even in his grandmother's room. They always shooed him away like there was a disease in the room's air he might catch. But he knew what they were talking about.

In the narrow lanes of north Calcutta, Trinankur was a natural growth, a gnarled stem sprouted through chipped brickwork. Here he looked lost and hesitant, a big man who looked odd amidst the flock of shrieking boys. There was another man next to him. Manoj. Ori's father's friend from the same coil of lanes, a dark man with a balding forehead who smoked an endless number of cigarettes and often took Ori out to eat mishti at the local sweet shops. Ori was fond of Manoj. But he did not want to see him here in his school.

Quickly Ori sneaked out of their line of vision. He did not really need to. It would be hard for Trinankur or Manoj to find him in this horde of boys in white running around the school grounds and kicking up tiny dust storms.

Wandering around, the two men came closer. Ori's breath quickened. He slid behind one of the pillars in front of the school chapel. Two boys from Class One shot out noisily from somewhere and crashed into Trinankur's legs. Like grounded bugs, they flapped back to life and wrestled each other. Their shirts were yellow with fresh food stains, pickle oil or jelly. Trinankur looked stunned. A dark and plump middle-aged woman appeared from nowhere and screamed at the boys. Perhaps a nanny. Few people hated the little boys more than the nannies sent to fetch them from school.

Ori could get lost in this chaos of dust and shrieks and ravaged water bottles. They would never find him. But to try to flee was absurd. How could one run away from home? Slowly he stepped past the pillar, took a few steps toward the two men. His legs felt heavy.

"Oritro!" Trinankur's face glowed as his eyes fell on him. Quickly he walked toward Ori.

"We're here to take you home," he announced.

"Baba?" The word plopped out of Ori's mouth, wet and wilted.

"Baba's feeling a bit unwell." Manoj touched Ori's shoulder lightly. "We'll take you home."

Unwell was a word with a warm breath of fear. People whispered it and made late-night trunk calls between cities, sent urgent messengers with the word to snatch someone from sleep. The last part of their explanation was always a mumble, trailing off into silence.

"Hello, Oritro." Miss Miranda appeared, as if she had heard the trailing end of the sentence. "Is your father not here yet?"

The cracks widened on Trinankur's face. The tiny craters left by his pimples were lit up by a throbbing need to speak and no idea of what to say.

Silence sat there for a little while.

"Myself and Trinankur here, madam, we're from his neighbourhood," Manoj-kaku croaked hoarsely in English. *His* kind of English.

"He's the corporation councilor from the area," Manoj-kaku struggled on, pointing to Trinankur. "And I'm a close friend of Oritro's father."

Miss Miranda cast a quick glance at Trinankur. She always chatted with his father, whom Ori found a bit of a stranger in the presence of his class teacher. A likable stranger, as if he were playing a part in a movie. They both laughed a lot, and her eyes gleamed.

"We are knowing his family for a very long time," Trinankur said, thrusting forward his muscular shoulders, like he was about to plead for the vote of someone who did not understand his language. He rested a palm on Ori's shoulder. Ori felt the weight of his claim on his skin while an uneasy question fidgeted in his head. *Did Anglo-Indians vote for the Party?*

"His father not well. So we come to take him home."

"Not well?" Miss Miranda's forehead furrowed. "What's wrong with Mr. Basu?"

He was fine the last time he came after Ori's final exams. Last year. He and Miss Miranda had stood together chatting for five minutes at that time, questions over Ori's progress rippled with pleasant smiles.

"Miss," Manoj said, his voice dropping as he shot a quick glance at Ori.

"Come on." Trinankur took Ori aside. Manoj spoke to Miss Miranda, his voice falling to a whisper.

Ori looked away. Arvind was walking past with his mother, Mrs. Agarwal. She waved at him, and Arvind winked.

"Nice school," Trinankur murmured.

Ori half looked at Miss Miranda, unsure if he should. She was listening to Manoj. She appeared to hold her breath, suffocate a little.

"I understand," she said. "But we cannot let Oritro go off with you. It's against school policy."

Manoj-kaku said something. It seemed he could only whisper.

"I'm sorry, gentlemen, we cannot let the boy go with you," Miss Miranda said firmly. "But you could speak to the principal."

Father O'Flaherty's office was a high-ceilinged cave. Countless books were lined across the back walls, their thick spines inseparable from the mahogany knuckles of wall-built bookcases. The table was a maze of telephones—red and yellow lights, five different rings. Perched behind them was the gaunt face of the Irish priest.

"Gentlemen, this is terrible news," he said. "But I don't see how we can let the boy go off with someone his parents have not officially authorized to escort him home after school."

They had never tried harder in their lives. Not Trinankur, to win the votes of people who found his pimples annoying. Nor Manoj-kaku, to convince people of whatever he was always trying to convince them of at street corners and tea stalls. It's a family in a very difficult situation and how can you say no, Father? They looked sharply at Ori. Palms were splayed out, and foreheads became shiny with sweat. Rules are rules, gentlemen, and even I can't break school policy.

But he couldn't let the boy stand in the school yard all night, could he? Neither of his parents were coming to pick him up today. Not to be expected, not after what he heard from Miss Miranda. Quick glance at the boy, now biting his nails hard, maybe to draw blood out of them? No, hold back all my visitors, Gomez, I'm in the middle of a serious problem. How about a telephone call? Could they get someone to come on the phone and authorize these gentlemen to take the boy away from the school? Miss Miranda, can you make the call?

Miss Miranda's long nails dipped into the digit holes and dialed. Grrrrrrrrrr. Six times. The rattling noise slipped a noose around everybody; all fell silent. In the rattle-struck silence, Ori's mind boarded a crowded minibus and went home, sat cross-legged before the tiny marble-topped table in the corner of the hall, heard the black telephone ring on top of it. Krrrrrrrng. Six times. Back in the principal's room, he realized someone had picked up the phone at home, heard Miss Miranda say into the receiver that she was Oritro's class teacher speaking from Saint P's College. Her voice was sweet as a lullaby, not a voice they ever heard in class. Faint furrows ridged her forehead. Maya had picked up the phone. To her, Miss Miranda's lullaby English was a malfunction of the receiver. Miss Miranda paused, the furrows melting into something emptier, blanker. After a few seconds, she mouthed "Hello" again. Repeated the soft lullaby sentence. All over again.

"It's an old lady," she spoke to the room. "Someone needs to talk to her in Bengali."

Quickly the peon Gomez fetched Mr. Saha, the Bengali teacher from the senior school. Out there before the marble-topped table, Mummum took charge and Mr. Saha began to melt, politeness oozing off his voice. Yes, Mashima; no, of course not, Mashima, rest assured! Mr. Saha thanked her profusely and promised her that Ori would be home soon. Father O'Flaherty, beginning to feel the mounting pressure of demands outside his door, looked relieved now that Ori would not have to spend the night on his office sofa. Miss Miranda seemed unconvinced by the whole business. She was going to grill Mr. Saha later as to what was said on the phone. Mr. Saha would be only too happy to tell her everything.

Trinankur and Manoj-kaku shot out of the office like freshly wound toys, grabbing Ori by the hand. No telling when the Father Saheb might change his mind again. Outside the grounds, now cleaned of mothers and drivers and ravaged water bottles, had a mournful kind of emptiness. There were just a handful of the Catholic boys fooling around with a bat and a ball, boarders waiting for Father Wilson to take them to the hostel, a fifteen-minute walk away. As he stepped out, Ori heard a familiar metallic groan: the school sentry was swinging shut one of the hinges of the heavy blue school gate.

15

At the entrance to Trinankur's house was a shrine. From the grime of the pavement, you stepped into a fragrant swathe of marble. Having made a fortune from a mustard-oil dealership, Trinankur had enshrined in marble a prophet from suburban Bengal who had gathered many followers long before death had turned him into a god. At the heart of the shrine sat the marble bust of the old man with a knotty beard and a kind smile that calmed you.

A pale boy with close-cropped hair sat on a wheelchair inside the marble hall. A boy with a happy grin and slurred speech. A smiling Buddha on a throne. He was Subhankar, Trinankur's son and only child, a boy born with a rare disease. A rare but persistent disease that ate up his muscles, a little every year. All the way, the doctors had agreed, till he was sixteen when all his muscles would be gone. That gave him six more years to live. He was a stocky boy, always with a friendly smile. Last year he had eased into a wheelchair. He could not walk anymore. He was wheeled along the bumpy lanes of the neighbourhood by his mother, a pale woman with rich hair and a square face. Sometimes it was his father, the local leader of the Party.

Trinankur was an important man. You went to him if you had a problem. That is if you were clever. If not, you went to the police, where flies buzzed over tea in chipped cups while the officers stretched out with their feet on their desks. But people in the para were clever and so Trinankur was a very, very busy man. He cut red ribbons to inauguarate new clubs and tapes over forgotten files to clear overdue pensions and the delivery of cooking-gas cylinders. When tenants fought with landlords they went to his office and his boys came and banged on the landlord's doors. If the landlord was clever he also went to Trinankur and then the matter was settled in the Party office. If he was stupid and went to the Congress Party, the back alleys filled with battle.

Trinankur and his wife were like parents to the para. Some people said this was because their own son was not going to live for long. A few years back, when Ori was younger, a question fidgeted endlessly in his head: would Trinankur and his wife tear down the marble shrine when their boy died? Like a Durga Puja *pandal* after Dashami, the end of the big festival?

Now he knew they wouldn't. Trinankur's wife wasn't the kind of person who tore things down. Everything about this pale, heavyset woman sagged just a little bit from the weight of kindness, as if she were a ripe sandesh made of cottage cheese that was now going faintly sour. A sad life had made her kinder to the world.

Ori smiled at Subhankar. "Why don't you stay here awhile, play with Subhankar?" Trinankur said and vanished into the house. But how did one play with Subhankar, who could not even get up from his wheelchair? He had a huge pile of books and comics resting on a little recessed shelf attached to his chair, a mobile playhouse. And he wanted you to have them all. The wilted generosity of a life cut short. Did he know it himself?

"I have to go home," Ori murmured.

A shadow clouded Subhankar's mother's cottage-cheese face. "Why? Don't you like it here?" she asked.

How could he not, with the spread before him? Fresh *parathas* shiny with ghee, a spicy *alur dom*, the small, round potatoes with gentle bald heads soaked in gravy. Well-browned, happy. Three different kinds of sweets. Steamed, fried, and syrupy. All that a boy wanted after a long day at school.

They could not understand why he wanted to go home.

"Eat," she said. "I know you're hungry."

But it was not a house that gave answers. Why Ori couldn't go home. Why his parents would still not come to pick him up. Why could he not just go around the block and knock at his own front door? There were no answers. Trinankur was gone and his kind wife only asked him to eat and worry about nothing. Subhankar stared at him with his happy eyes and kept smiling.

Nobody would say anything. Till Trinankur's brother Dushtu stepped into the holy marble. He took off his weathered rubber slippers and left them in the corner of the hall. His leathery face looked wrinkled. "What the bloody hell is the world coming to?" his voice hissed. "How does a boy from a decent home suddenly become homeless?"

"What do you mean, homeless?" Subhankar's mother protested. "Rupa-Boudi has the family under her wings, and she'll let no harm touch the boy.

"And we're not dead yet; can't we look after him for a while?" Her voice trembled.

Dushtu snapped back. "Boudi, but he does have parents, doesn't he? Or had them, sort of. You pull a hard enough burden." He pointed to Subhankar, happily flipping through the pages of *Tintin* with curry-stained fingers.

"My son is no burden, whatever he is." The doughy sweetness of her face tightened to a bitter crust. "And you have no shame at all, saying such things in front of the children, your own nephew too!"

"Whatever he is." Dushtu cast a sharp look at Ori, who toyed with the torn pieces of luchi on his plate. "This boy is no longer a child." He paused. "He's seen more than Subhankar will in his whole life."

It was as if someone took the soft sandesh face of Subhankar's mother and flung it against the wall to pulp.

Dushtu hissed, "Who would have thought things would come to this today?"

"Why do men do *nasha*?" the soft sandesh woman whispered. "Such strange *nasha* when they just lie dead for hours?"

"Why would he care?" Dushtu asked. "Why stay awake to suffer when your wife has her heart outside home?"

Suddenly Ori wanted nothing more than to sit on Subhankar's chair, have someone wheel him around. It was a nasty wish. Not even the little kids of the para cried for a ride on Subhankar's chair. Everybody knew. But right now, Ori would do anything to be taken around in that chair, wheels crunching over eggshells spilled from the garbage heaps, while he leafed through the pages of *Tintin* and *Asterix* piled high in his little chair nook, chewing on strawberry-flavored bubble gum. For five, no maybe three years. After the disease had eaten up the muscles, the last couple of years had to be spent chewing gum in bed. That is, if the jaws could still move.

He closed his eyes.

"Ori!"

She was here. Shruti. She was here to wheel him around, through the crooked lanes of the para. Over the mushy skin of rotting vegetables and the crunchy shells of eggs. Sitting in the chair, he could feel the slow energy of the steps behind it. She knew where to take him.

And then he looked up to her and his heart stopped beating.

Her hair was tousled and eyes glazed with confusion. Sweaty confusion with a fine patina of fear. It sat uneasy on her end-of-the-college-day fatigue; it shone along her long, smooth arms and showed up in the stickiness of her seaweed green kurta clinging to her body. She wore the same old pair of blue jeans, faded at the knees.

"Ori." Shruti strode up to the table and held his hand, gently at first, and then so tight that it hurt. "Come with me."

Subhankar's mother spoke up sharply. "He's not going anywhere. Now's not the time to take a child to that house." Anger sat on her face like an open wound.

Dushtu stood there in silence. His dead eyes bore into Shruti.

"He'll stay right here," Subhankar's mother said, tremors running through her voice. "My husband is responsible for him. The Party will decide when it's safe for him to go home."

"This is no business for a young girl," Dushtu said now, his voice shaking with anger.

Shruti said nothing. She walked to a corner, picked up Ori's school satchel and water bottle.

"He's coming home," she said. Her voice was quiet. She glanced sharply at Ori. "Come on, let's go."

As they left, anger hung inside the marbled shrine like a bad odour.

Out on the street, Ori throbbed with questions.

"Why didn't Baba come to school to pick me up?"

"Where is Baba?"

"Where is Ma?"

Shruti took her usual long strides. "Tata is feeling unwell," she said without slowing down. Without looking at him.

Tata had remained her baby name for Ori's father, the man who had taught baby Shruti to let go of people she hated to see go away.

"Not feeling well like evening?" Ori asked.

Most evenings were not part of his father's life. They were sliced and destroyed. Into hours of sleep behind bolted doors, soon after his mother left, fragrant and beautiful. Sometimes he would rouse himself for dinner, to look with bloodshot eyes at the roti he took forever to tear into bite-sized pieces.

"Like the evening," Shruti replied. "Today it was evening all day."

Ahead they could see the main door of their house.

They would not slow down. But he *had* to ask before they stepped inside.

Shruti looked away. "Rima has gone. She took all her things." Her voice shook. "*Everything.*"

※

Inside the house, the air felt raw. Nobody spoke but you could hear the strained breathing of tight-lipped people. The door to Mummum's room was closed. The maidservants moved around with bruised looks. Everybody seemed to burrow away in some corner or the other the moment they saw him enter the house with Shruti.

As he entered his parents' bedroom, his eyes shot to the dressing table. There was a huge gash in the dressing mirror where the glass was gone. Bare, reddish wood stared back at him like a stale wound. The rest of the glass was cracked.

Darkness hugged the room like an old blanket with holes. Holes through which yellow patches of the afternoon entered the room and caressed his father's body, rising and falling on the bed with a drawn-out, wheezing sound. His arms and legs were spread out, like he'd suddenly been trapped in a fishnet while swimming underwater. He, too, was gone from this world. Faintly, his chest rose and fell on the bed, a rippling slab of earth, keeping time with the streaming whir of the ceiling fan. Standing in the darkness of the room, Ori felt the rhythm enter his own body, swallow it up.

Evening was here. Here to stay.

The dark, claustrophobic room, with the shuttered windows took Ori floating back into the past. It was a past where breathing was difficult, like air dense with floating animal hair. Where he was trapped, a small child, as his parents clawed at each other in a senseless haze of violence with the door locked from within. A room stale and battered with pain. He looked at the heaving body of his father on the bed. Shruti stood on the threshold. Her eyes followed the trail of violence in the room, the anger still knotted and crumpled inside the bedclothes. "Glass splinters were all over the place. They fought so violently that the neighbours rushed into the room," she whispered. "And then the Party people turned up."

"That murderer Tatai was here," she gasped with rage. "Talking like a school principal. *The Party has taken a lot of trouble to clean up the city and wipe out the bar and cabaret singers on Park Street and we'll not let this old and refined neighbourhood be soiled by women who come home in the dead of night with paint on their faces, no, never, the Party will not stand for it. You stay here if you can stay a decent woman.* He hisses at her face. Can you believe it?" Her eyes welled up with tears. "The man who used to be a contract killer before he joined the Party?

"*Or you can pack your bags and get the hell out of here.*" Her voice fell to a whisper. "The bastard, I wanted to punch his face. I would've done it if he wasn't with the Party."

Suddenly she was jolted back to the real. Fear clouded her face. She crossed the threshold and slipped into the room.

Stiffly she took him in her arms. He smelled metallic fragrance brushed with a whiff of cigarette smoke. Filter Wills.

All at once, his muscles wilted. He touched the sweat-dampened back of her kurta. At long last, she needed him.

16

The cinema halls dotting Shyambazar and Hatibagan took up Ahin's afternoons and evenings. Sometimes he even had to sit through a show. The dark held the hint of promising bodies caught in the spell of the movie, sharp with excitement, sleepy with love, resting on a beloved shoulder to the right. Characters appeared in his mind through the way they came to possess or surrender armrests, whistled at the screen, ordered popcorn. Through the way they arched their bodies backward to let the latecomer shuffle past and reach his seat.

Even more promising were the lobby and the street that swelled with the waiting crowd. The crowd grew colourful from the matinee onward and climaxed with the carnival of the evening show. Chattering powdered housewives, fresh from their evening bath, sheepish schoolboys, lovers who cared not in the least about the movie but merely hungered for the dark, the only place in the city where they could hold hands in secret.

It was a sea of people from which Ahin just needed six bodies. Rushing through crowds, his eyes scanned faces and ankles and curling fingers, running out of breath, falling into a trance, floating past promising faces and dreamlike voices.

But nothing was quite real, touchable. None of these bodies would quite give in. Always they laughed and twitched and wriggled beyond his reach. Sometimes he despaired of bringing the play to life. But to give up the dream was to stop breathing.

They laughed at him these days, at Ahin Mullick whose silk kurta, once regal, was now splotched with betel juice, the last soul from the ancient family in Hatibagan who had owned the most glittering playhouse of Calcutta. Men who bedded the prettiest actresses and paid for their glitz. What silken days! The British still owned companies in Dalhousie Square then and firang dancers frolicked in Grand and Great Eastern and you drank Pink Lady and White Lady in Firpo's and Trinca's and Magnolia's to glowing music and cabaret crooners, the same crooners who spiced up the plays that drew the crowds to Indralok and Rangmahal and Minerva. Silken days they were.

The scum! They called him crazy.

But he knew a body made for the stage if he saw one, sniffed its scent, or touched it in the dark. Something about its skin, smooth and slippery and shape-defying. Something about the way it moved, as if its life in daylight was simply a long wait in the wings. Especially if it didn't know it yet.

Like the little boy, shaking with fear and longing in the dark end of the theatre as his mother rehearsed for a raunchy role.

"Fifty for twenty." The lanky bootlegger of movie tickets popped up before Ahin.

"Don't need any," Ahin muttered. His mind floated back to a stilted chat, a memory of reaching out and touching shy fingers in the dark.

Little boys and girls came to the theatres from time to time, looking for their mothers. Mothers who were busy wrapping sari ends around waists to do a dance number, mothers running after characters with makeup kits, mothers who tended hair and brushed wigs to perfection.

Meera, too, had a son. A son who might appear in a dark silk shirt under the yellow light of the brothel.

Meera. The smell of her body would shape the play.

Meera. Sometimes the despair became real. Reality that surrounded, held, and cupped him. That Meera would never come. Look him in the face. Live the life carved for her. *Never.*

Rocket and Bullet, the swaggering duo of pimps who slid in and out of the wings like a pair of venomous lizards, tongues shooting out at the faintest scent of prey.

"Forty for twenty." The young bootlegger came back, looked at Ahin out of the corner of his eye. A swaggering boy with a smooth upper lip, touched with a razor a few years too soon.

"Go away," Ahin said. Impatiently.

The young bootlegger's face flashed open in a quick snarl. A carnivore, suddenly baring its fangs, quickly drawing them back. The hint of brutality came and went in a flash. Singed by his hot breath, suddenly Ahin stared at him, mesmerized.

"I'll give it to you for the price at which I bought it." The bootlegger pulled out the ticket, a crumpled piece of orange paper, a conjurer pulling out magic. "Deal?"

Tidal waves crashed through Ahin's head. Armies galloped. It was a ticking time bomb, the bootlegger's unseasonably shaved skin. He *was* Bullet. The poisoned youth that lived in his dreams.

"You're the pimp!" He grabbed the boy's shirtfront, crumpling the skin around his neck in an iron fist, crushing it to pulp. "You *are!*" he screamed.

Bullet had snarled to life. The snake of a killer who would cast his cold shadow over Lila after Meera fled the brothel, a cold shadow over her dreams of freedom, of a new life preparing and bottling pickles that would make men's mouths water just as her body had.

The bootlegger's fist exploded against Ahin's face like a tiny bomb. It was a fist proudly crested by a row of metal rings. Ahin's lips oozed salty blood mixed with betel juice. He reeled and crumpled against the wall, the weight of his body tearing down a giant cutout from the movie about to start soon.

"Pimp?" screamed the young bootlegger, raising another knotted fist. "*Saala* harami! Me a pimp! *Me?*"

People gathered around Ahin as the final bell announced the beginning of the movie inside. Like a harried father, the hall manager burst through the crowd.

"Out of my hall!" he shrieked at the bootlegger with bloodstained, betel-juiced knuckles. "Bloody hero, bashing up that loony!"

Ahin felt lightning scorch his eyelids. A fine blue hair of lightning. A needle of shooting pain.

It happened every time they called him a loony.

17

Walking out with all her things, his mother left the maze of crooked lanes far behind and rented a house in a suburb on the southern edge of Calcutta.

He had barely finished his first week in Class Six when she turned up at his school and took him away, all the way to a newly rented house thick with the odour of dust and new paint, lime-green, so bright and raw that it hurt your eyes, right in the middle of tiled roofs over makeshift wooden houses selling soda and bubble gum. It was a stretch of land that was trying to enter Calcutta, a township of plowed fields and naked railway tracks eager to become part of the city.

It was the beginning of an odd life. He left school alone these days and came back to his new home. But it was a new home that had quickly started to decay. Paint and varnish jobs remained unfinished and wooden windows stayed bare, like rattling, hideous parts of skeletons. His mother was like a little girl. She did not know how to make a home, go grocery shopping, set up a larder and cook real meals, keep the servant and the cleaning woman from cheating. Bills and receipts and budgets refused to make sense to her. She had never done any of it before. Life remained scattered for months. Boxes were not unpacked; meals were skipped. Running between rehearsals, she could not separate day and night, afternoon and evening. Plays written and Xeroxed in coarse sheets and cheap notebooks littered the home, bit roles in them marked with green highlighters.

His mother went on long treks all over the city, trying to meet directors and producers who were *never* at home when she knocked on their doors, people who had promised to send for her but never did, offered dreams of new productions that never got off the ground. There were small-time productions stifled by their own poverty, trapping her in gnawing worry over money that she rarely got. She didn't have time to catch her breath, much less to go drop off and pick up her son from school every day.

All of a sudden, Ori was free to wander alone in the city. The school bus did not come to his new home. He walked right past the school gates; the air smelled different, reeked of the anger and exhaustion of the masses through whom he had to fight his way. The walk went on forever, past tracks over which ancient trams thundered, all the way to the whirl of the train station. The vastness of the station burst with the hum of a million voices, endless people squatting on the platforms. The crowd in the coaches like live chickens in a basket, the tunnel of rotting-leather stench the train passed through each day. The jaunty rhythm of the rickshaw ride to an empty house that reeked of dust and paint.

It was an odd house. Strange things stood out in it. A blonde woman smiled at him from a cardboard box of books and magazines at the corner of the bathroom. A box yet to be unpacked. The woman smiled at him as he sat on the potty, her pale, naked shoulders shining at him like peeled, water-streaked fruits.

It was the cover of a book with well-thumbed corners. Well-thumbed, he knew, by his baba who sometimes hid American paperbacks with tiny, tiny print and forbidden covers behind the cricket magazines he pretended to read. A near-naked woman who had come with his ma's things by mistake.

A tingle through his stomach had got his bowels moving. Fast. Afterward he would take the woman out, his fingers touching the well-thumbed corners, raising a small puff of dust. Mesmerized, he would stare at her naked stomach, tapered like the middle of an expensive vase, at the cruel playfulness on her face. Hide her back in the cardboard box so that no one could say she had smiled at him.

The woman who made him go to the toilet several times a day, causing a fine flutter in his bowels every time.

Odd, odd things, like the smell of dust and new paint that never left the house no matter how much his mother tried to wear it down, make it a house lived in.

❧

The months passed. A smoky mist floated over the township through the winter months that disappeared as summer drew near. You could now see for miles, so that you realized that there was nothing to see but dusty scaffoldings of houses yet unbuilt and vast ponds choked with water hyacinths.

Ori returned from school one afternoon to find faces from the old neighbourhood in the house. There was Rupa, Trinankur, and a couple of other people—Mala, a loud, bullying woman from the citizens' council and one of his father's cousins, a hesitant older man who looked like he didn't want to be there. They had shown up at the door like a strange dream from the ancient, crooked lanes.

Ori found it hard to believe that it was really Rupa. She always liked to keep a distance from others' lives. She would laugh drily, muttering that her sister-in-law could go to her own hell if she wanted, nobody would care to stop her. What had made her come all this way, pick out this makeshift address in this half-baked housing colony on the edge of the city? Fear and joy fought each other in his mind.

They questioned everything, sniffing at the air in the house as if a dead animal had been rotting there in some hidden corner. Maybe it was the smell of dust and new paint that drove them crazy, or maybe the way the kitchen cabinets were stuffed with packets of Maggi noodles. Mala-di, the woman from the Party, wanted to take the house apart with her sharp, suspicious nose. Ori knew her well—she was a disheveled, chatty woman who visited every house in the para to persuade the women to pay their dues for the women's wing of the Party.

"Doesn't look like you cook anything, Garima," Rupa remarked. "What do you feed the boy?"

His mother stared at Rupa. "You have some cheek," she said softly.

Rupa stormed past her and barged into the bedroom. She stared at the windswept beds by the window opening into the wilderness. "The mosquitoes here are deadly, like tiny fighter jets," she muttered. No bedposts anywhere to hang mosquito nets from, no mosquito nets anywhere.

"What do you expect? This is just a refugee colony," Mala remarked. "People are still clearing the bushes and draining the water."

"You're really trying to get the boy malaria, aren't you?" Suddenly, Rupa's voice faltered. "He looks thin and sickly enough."

His mother fought them with a ferocity that scared Ori and made his heart ache. She was like a troubled child locked in a frenzy of jagged violence against the world.

"Have you seen the open drains?" Rupa had hissed. "Fertile breeding ground for malaria mosquitoes. He can't stay here."

There was fear in his mother's eyes as she looked at her sister-in-law. "He must come back home. He must." Rupa's voice was as hard as steel.

Without straining his ears, Ori could hear his Mummum's voice seep through his aunt's words. An old woman with cold eyes. A soft, doughy voice that sprinkled ice on your skin. The battle lines were raw. He was the son of the family. The bearer of the family name, the boy with the same fair skin and lanky build that belonged to his father, and to his grandfather before him. The boy who was the future. His mother didn't matter. She could go if she wanted to. Nobody cared. But she could not take the boy away. He wasn't hers.

His mother's grip tightened around his arm like a pair of steel pincers.

"You think you can keep him?" Rupa hissed. "Water does not crawl upward. A boy will return to his family."

Then they had left, the door ajar behind them, the dusty wind streaming inside.

18

The big change came around the beginning of Class Seven. Life at home suddenly became a secret in school, a kind of nothingness about which he could not talk. He let everyone slip out of people's memory—his parents, Mummum, even Shruti, and it was strange how easily they were forgotten by his friends, even the teachers who liked to talk to him.

He walked out of the school gates at the end of the day as quietly as possible so that few people noticed that he went home alone. It was still a little strange in Class Seven, and other parents sometimes looked at him with curiosity, while he slipped away quickly, warmth creeping behind his ears. He wanted to disappear into a world no one knew about, a world that almost did not exist.

That afternoon he had just stepped out of the school gates when a bony hand gripped his shoulder from behind. Fear wriggled in his stomach. He was trapped!

"School is over?"

Ahin Mullick smiled at him.

"Yes," Ori said, his throat dry.

Why was this man here? Did his mother send him? To take him home? But why? He went home alone every day.

"Let's go." The man's hand slid down Ori's shoulders, and rested on his back, taking over his body.

Ori looked at the man, not knowing what to say. He hated being around this man. He was everywhere. It was hard to be around a rehearsal or a performance in north Calcutta where he didn't show up, smile sitting on his face, his fingers reaching out to pinch Ori's cheeks or ruffle his hair. He had a strange affection for Ori. It nauseated Ori and somehow managed to dilute his hatred. Nobody seemed to notice the man lurking in the wings of the stage or in the corner of a rehearsal room. But his greasy smile stirred a raw memory. Sensation that did not bear thinking about.

Heat flashed through his brain as he walked ahead briskly. The weird man would get lost easily behind him.

The lane narrowed ahead, shadowed by the cluster of balconies leaning out of old houses standing cheek by jowl. Questions rattled in his head as he walked. Did his mother send him? But why him?

"Listen!" A singsongy voice chased him. "Stop. I will take you home."

Ori's ears became warm. The man was shouting! People would stop and stare.

"Sweetie." The man's voice came closer. Warmly it breathed on Ori's shoulders.

Ori slowed down. Together they entered the darkness of the tunnel that ran between the houses. Puppies scurried around their feet and rubbed up against their ankles. As they entered the dark, the man's palm touched Ori's back. It rubbed his skin softly, as if afraid of losing him in the darkness. Travelling along his elbow, the palm now grasped his thin wrist. Ori walked along, undeterred, maintaining a steady pace, unmoved from his path.

The man knew the way. Out on the main street, he turned right. Together they slipped through the muddle on the pavement, through the chanting of the vendors.

Was he hungry? Ahin asked. *Would he like to eat anything?*
No. Ori wasn't hungry.
But it is a long, long walk to Sealdah station!
Yes, it is.

Ori stole a quick glance at Ahin's face, suddenly reassured that the man did, indeed, know the way to his house. And how else would he know if Ori's mother didn't tell him? Why else would he come here if she didn't ask him? But why him?

But odd things made up his mother's new life. Unpacked boxes with naughty paperback books buried in them. A windswept, empty house with the smell of paint and dust. Odd visitors popped in and out. A landlord who looked like an aging wrestler. Yoga teachers who dropped in at odd hours. Masseuses, hairdressers, and makeup women who came in to sob about their lives, the men they loved and hated. Days and nights afloat in chaos, the barren odour of dust and disappointment hanging over their brittle, toy home. Odd, odd things.

The man was scared of the dark. As they entered the giant market under the Sealdah flyover, he appeared afraid, afraid of the gloom obscuring his vision, afraid of losing Ori to the underground maze of slime and vegetables. In the patchy darkness of the market, his hand roamed again. It climbed down Ori's satchel, skimming hastily over the pointy spines of bound books, and sought the soft fragility of his spine, the hollow of his lower back, the rough skin of his elbow. His words were a shy whisper.

"You've acted before, haven't you?"

"No. Never." There was shame in Ori's voice. The only time he had stepped under the spotlight, it was to feign sleep under the violence of clashing swords. But pretending to sleep on stage was not acting.

"You can," the man said and stopped, a statue breathing among piles of vegetable skin, beggar children scampering like stray kittens. He pulled Ori by the wrist, brought him close. *Closer.* He touched Ori's face, a blind man trying to see. Coarse fingers curled into his cheeks, his sharp, slightly crooked nose, his arched mouth. They crawled over his lips, parted them. Ori tasted dust on the fingers, and the leprous hardness of calluses. Reviled, he wanted to spit but could not unfreeze his body. "What you are, you have no idea," Ahin whispered. He pinched Ori's lips, his gnarled fingers melting into their softness. "You have no idea at all . . . of what you can do!" The gnarled hand crawled down his chin, cupped it. Slid under the collar of his shirt.

Stricken, Ori flung the hand off. Whirling around, he ran through the crooked lane between mounds of potatoes and porters in loincloths with spines crooked under their loads. Fearfully toward the train station.

"Careful on the streets." The man trotted behind him, pecking at the air with his pointy mouth. "And run for the 4:49 Canning Local."

"You never buy tickets, right?" he asked as they strode through the hall onto the giant stretch of platforms.

His words shot right through Ori! The money Ma gave him every day for tickets lay unused, toward funds for something big, like a treat for a dozen boys at school. *How did the man know?*

A jolt and a chill, the faintest of chills, went up his spine. At the back of his neck, it grew wings and flew away.

They boarded the train together. "You can," the man murmured as the train raced past the Park Circus tanneries, its solid tunnel of stench, "make slaves of them all, right here in this train. What you are," he paused, looking at a vendor of ointments snake his slow, sure way through the flesh-packed corridor, "you have no idea. Look at that idiot." His voice rose on "idiot," high enough for a couple of people to stare, and Ori wanted to slip away, vanish in shame through the floor of the train, into the speeding tracks underneath. "You can sell his wares to the whole crowd in half the time he takes to sell to three people in the compartment. All you have to do is to go up there and be yourself." A smile twinkled in his eyes. Ori let his eyes float toward the vendor, the middle-aged man in white shirt and gray trousers moving through the train, displaying his stuff to commuters.

"I don't know . . ." Ori lisped, the sound dying on his lips, unable to shut off the lights sparkling in his brain.

"Your mother winces when I tell her," Ahin said, spreading out his gnarled palms helplessly. "Actresses don't want their children to act. They never do." He laughed. "Especially when their children are beautiful."

They inched their way to the door of the crowded compartment. Entering Dhakuria station, the train slowed down.

And then suddenly, without warning, everything changed. The colour of the sky and the feel of the air. The trance shattered. Right as they stepped off the train, the moment Shruti walked up to them on the platform.

"Got you!" she whistled. "I know you take the 4:49!"

Her familiar blue salwar was a flash of colour in the sea of people crowding the drab platform. Ori's heart swelled with an aching joy. Nervously, he tried to throttle it, clip its wild wings. A flurry of emotions fought each other. Dizzying anger. Breathless resentment. Love that melted your bones, your inner organs, and made you weightless.

And Ahin Mullick . . . He was a statue left behind by the train rumbling away to Canning. A statue frozen in shock. Staring in shocked disbelief.

At Shruti.

19

Ahin Mullick stood on the platform till the blast of the next train hit him full on the face. Absently, he boarded it. The train that sped in the wrong direction, farther and farther away from his home.

He didn't realize that he was in the wrong train. He didn't notice the overpowering smell of raw fish that clouded his compartment.

His mind was already home. In his room above the magic playhouse where paint and plaster crumbled daily onto the floor. Gently, his mind slipped under his pillow and caressed the sheaf of long, browned sheets with brittle edges, lines of handwriting running across them. Right through the directions that narrowed the spotlight on Meera's heartachingly beautiful face. Of the tall man of shrouded face who would not go away, the pleasures he wrenched out of Meera's body like a wet towel being wrung dry. The stranger left her body drained and her sari's anchal bloated with bundles of crisp banknotes every evening, all through the long weeks that her husband, Mrinmoy, was away driving cargo to Amritsar and Chandigarh and Delhi. It gave birth to the first lie in their marriage, to explain away the pack of imported cigarettes left under the bed, a glossy, black pack. She liked the mild, dry whiff of the foreign cigarettes, she told Mrinmoy, and had picked up the pack at a shop. Meera. The soul of *Dusk*.

Without Meera, *Dusk* did not exist. Without *Dusk*, Meera was nothing.

Meera, who had walked up the station platform in a blue salwar, blinding Ahin as he stood not five steps from the train. Canning Local 4:49. With lazy steps, she had walked toward him. To touch his life with the smell of dusk draped around her body. Just as he had dreamt, always.

Meera could not be sought out. You could not walk the streets looking for her. You had to wait.

He had waited. And Meera had come.

The softness of Mrinmoy's smile hid more than it revealed. The man who could love much more than he showed. He asked no questions, but his smile grew, softer, richer, a river in high tide. But it revealed not even a fragment of the love he was capable of.

The beautiful nightmare of the last scene! Meera stood at the edge of an abyss. The smooth, rounded abyss in the heart of the circular auditorium of The Pantheon. Madly, the lit bulb of her face flew around the round crater left gaping by the sunken stage. But she could not flee Mrinmoy's love. On the rising stage, Mrinmoy was a tall shadow. As the stage filled out the rounded abyss, he cradled her swanlike neck in the crook of his arm, and loved her, deep and long, squeezing air out of her throat till she bucked like the headless body of a freshly slaughtered chicken, to come to peace in his arms. Slowly life ebbed out of her as dreamy light danced on the auditorium's circular wall.

Lovingly he braided the dead woman's hair into a long, thick plait, noosed it around her neck like a hangman's knot. Her lovely flesh and luxuriant hair had killed her.

Speeding toward the Bay of Bengal amidst a cloud of stinking fish, Ahin reeled from the shock of seeing Meera in the flesh. For the first time ever, with his eyes wide open.

She was walking along the platform, walked up to him, smiling at Ahin.

Meera.

20

"How do you go home?" Shruti asked as they walked out of the train station. "Rickshaw?"

"Yeah," Ori murmured as they approached the rickshaw stand.

"Come." Shruti pulled his wrist gently as the first rickshaw-wallah in the line looked at them.

Awkwardly, Ori muttered directions to him. He felt odd doing it while Shruti stood beside him, saying nothing.

He had only seen her a few times this past year, during the times he had gone to visit his father and grandmother in the old neighbourhood. They had not met elsewhere. And she had never come to visit them here.

She always acted as if home did not exist, that her real life was in the swelling ecstasy of her college and friends. That she had nothing to do with the shrieking mess of her home.

"Is Rima home?" she asked.

"Don't know," he shrugged.

They lapsed into silence. There was only the grating noise of the rickshaw. The cycle-drawn rickshaw made a sleeker, kinder noise than the hand-pulled rickshaws of north Calcutta, which Ori hated, their jagged, noisy dance, the heavy breathing of the rickshaw puller between the jaunty movements of the wheels.

Had she just come to see his mother? What about him?

Ducks quacked. The absurdity of the sound struck at the silence but it refused to dissolve.

The questions tossed and turned inside. But he could not break the silence.

"Ori?" Shruti asked, looking at the ducks lolling around in the pond. "Do you like this place?"

"Yes," he said, looking away. "It's okay."

He couldn't think of anything else to say. This was another universe. It felt raw and open, too full of sunlight, too many tiled roofs over makeshift wooden huts that sold soda and bubble gum, unplastered houses with bricks naked on them.

Their new house had plaster and paint on it. Lime-green paint.

He asked the rickshaw-wallah to stop. Quickly he counted out the change and handed it to him before Shruti could reach for her purse. From his pocket, he took out the keychain. A single key on a chain, attached to a seashell with a serrated mouth, to open the heavy lock at the door. One key for his mother and one for him.

He hated opening the lock, the grating noise of the key inside the hole, the way it clicked the lock open. He avoided Shruti's eyes. A lightning flash of anger sped through him. Why was she here? Why had she come to see him in this bare, poor house? Cautiously he passed through the little living space with the large open window overlooking the forest of weeds and bitter leaves, the maroon sofa from the old house that looked homeless here. Sand grated under the soles of their feet. Dust gathered fast in this house, dust and sand and dry specks of cement that always flew around in the air in these parts, a township fighting wilderness in order to be born.

"Ori,?" Shruti asked, "When will Rima be back?"

"Don't know," he said. "Why?"

"I want to talk to her."

"Why?"

"*Why?*" She looked at him strangely. "You wouldn't understand."

"Why?" he asked.

"Never mind." Quickly she gathered herself. "Are you hungry?"

"A little," he shrugged. He opened the door to the fridge and took out the loaf of sliced bread. The Amul salted butter was where he'd left it yesterday, on the top right shelf.

"Bread and butter? Now?" Shruti's voice echoed disbelief. "How about *lunch*?"

"It's too late." Roughly he shut the fridge door. "Who has lunch at five thirty?"

"You've got to be out of your mind," she said, her voice etching with exasperation, "to have bread and butter at the end of a whole day at school."

What's it to you? He wished he could say that. Instead he looked away from the stale yellow world inside the refrigerator and met her eyes. He hated her look. Her eyes peeped right inside him.

Propped half-open with his elbow, the refrigerator smelt of stale food. Old, old milk, uneaten paratha from last week, the remains of instant noodles from no one knew when. Butter frozen like yellow wax that would stubbornly resist the sharp edge of the knife.

Slowly he let go of the stale yellow world inside and let the door close shut.

"Oh, just forget about this!" She tugged at his arm. "Let's go out and eat something."

"Yes!" Suddenly his eyes shone.

He locked the house again, slipped the lone keychain with the serrated seashell back in his pocket, happy and free. They felt hungry for chicken-rolls. They combed the neighbourhood and laughed at the absurdity of seeking a roll-shack on streets that were not quite paved yet, streets flanked by patches of wilderness half-trimmed into football grounds where players fought tall wild grass to play. The afternoon grew milder, more pleasant, and she started talking. She wanted to ask her aunt to come back home. She *had* to come back. Nothing else mattered now. Tata and Rima always fought with each other, but how could Ori and Rima leave home just like that? The house felt cut open, left raw and blistered under the gaze of their neighbours. Everybody at home was bitter and quiet.

The house was quiet? Ori tried to imagine it. Aloud, he asked, "How is Mummum?" He kicked a roadside pebble, blowing up a tiny cloud of dust. He felt the sharp blow of shame. He wished he hadn't asked.

"Mummum?" Shruti asked absently. "She spends half the day looking for her keys that are tied to the anchal of her own sari before realizing where they are. No one knows what to make of her." Slow and silent, with the sickly thin black and white ribbon of hair down on her back, tied into a plait by Maya. *Only Maya.* Everything is strange. The para people march in and out of the house at all times. Trinankur and others from the Party. Tall, gaunt men in kurtas smelling of cigarette smoke, sleeves flecked with ash. Eyes roving. Dushtu and Tatai and the rest of the street muscle.

"Baba?" How was his father? Shruti looked away; her voice drooped. "My mother watches over him as though he's a little boy. When he's to eat and what he'll wear to the office the next day. The maids whisper but nobody says anything." Slowly Shruti brought her eyes back to meet Ori's. "Nothing like the house you know."

Her words slowed. Something tugged at Ori's heart, making it ache. The past. Things that had suddenly become the past. His bed in Mummum's room by the window. The sound of boys playing carom in the club right outside. Shruti. Who was here and was also in the past, not quite touchable.

They were lucky. There was a little shop near the train station stacked with Kwality ice cream and Coca-Cola and Limca and other fizzy drinks and writing paper and pens and instant noodles in shiny yellow packets.

The man took out little chicken patties from behind the shop's glass showcase, tiny yellow triangles of fried flour no one quite knew how old. And showed them to a narrow table and a couple of chairs just outside, touched by the fluorescent white light that lit up the little shop like a late-night factory.

"When I was a little girl," Shruti said, biting into a chicken patty, her mouth barely moving as she ate, "I used to say that I would marry Tata when I'm big."

They did not laugh. Ori, too, had faint memories of his father making fun of Shruti, then in her early teens, calling her *my shuo rani*, the better-loved, spoilt queen.

"But it was funny," she said, turning to him with a smile. "I was never ever jealous of Rima. I thought she was the most beautiful woman in the world. I'd stare and stare whenever she did her makeup. I knew the smell of every sari in her wardrobe."

Ori knew the stories. Once Shruti had tried to thread her eyebrows on her own, like his mother did, and had ended up bruising her skin. Rupa had locked her up in the unused kitchen near the servants' rooms for a whole day. Several days had passed before she spoke to Ori's mother again.

"I just want to talk to Rima," Shruti said. "Just talk."
Maybe she was back home by now?
Maybe. Ori could not tell.
They walked back to the lime-green house in silence. The lock still hung on the door. The house looked deserted.
It was almost dark. But Ori did not turn on the lights. The wan yellow light from the electric bulbs felt sadder than darkness in that lonely suburb while the crickets whirred from the tall grass outside.
A grimace appeared on Shruti's face. Ori followed her gaze to the wall. Right at the top, in the corner, a fat gray lizard was entangled with a thin yellow one. They looked dead but Ori knew they were not. A faint shiver passed through his body.
"What about you?" Shruti's voice groped in the dark. "Do you think about coming back home?"
He didn't know. It tired him to think. He remained silent.
"I should be getting back." Shruti glanced at her watch, a thin glint of silver across her wrist.
She would go away. Would she ever come again?
"Ma has a show in the north next weekend," Ori whispered. "Why don't you go and see her there after the play?"
"Where?" Shruti's voice sharpened.
"In The Pantheon. *A Midsummer Night's Dream.*"
"I could do that." Shruti's voice throbbed with excitement. "After the play."
"Yes," Ori said. "She will probably spend the night at Pallabi's house. The girl who does her hair. The show ends late and it's a long way from here."
"Tell Rima you'll spend the night with us that weekend." Shruti's voice had fallen to a whisper again. "We can talk afterward."
"Yes," Ori nodded eagerly, a warmth glowing inside him.
Shruti got up. They stepped out of the door again.

A rickshaw was the only way to get to the main road. To the world of buses and cars and taxis and bright lights, broad roads that were fully paved.

She waved at him from the rickshaw. Evening had set on her face. It looked dark. A face, he suddenly felt, he had trouble recognizing.

As the rickshaw trundled away, Ori's legs came back to life. Angry, violent life. He kicked at a pebble and sent it flying before sharply turning back in the direction of the lime-green house.

The key attached to the brown, serrated seashell poked through his pocket like a tiny, splintered bone.

21

The round stage was a toy forest with absurd curves and curlicues. It was a strange theatre, with the circular stage at its core that rose up and sank down between the scenes. Each new scene revealed a new forest of cheap streamers and ribbons rising slowly from the pit. Something about it, Shruti felt, was frail and childlike.

Music shuddered against the circular walls enclosing the audience gallery and verse floated across them. It was touching and magical and childish, all at the same time, the dancing and scurrying of lives on a stage like a small round plate in the heart of a near-empty hall. Where leaves fashioned out of coloured paper had created the woods just outside Athens.

Where the fairy met Puck, the spirit of the woods. Trickery flowed like blood through Puck's veins. Puck sang of Titania, the queen of the fairies, who sulked from her quarrel with Oberon, her king. He spoke and sang and danced and wreaked havoc with the language of life.

Shruti waited for Titania to appear.

It was for Titania that she had walked into this toy theatre, bought a ticket, seated herself in the desolate, near-empty audience gallery. Waiting, she heard a story she knew well, made alien by the lilt of Bengali verse. It was a story of stilled forest leaves, frozen bee wings, and the dead calm that throbbed in the forest with the anger of the king and the queen. Oberon and Titania. The throbbing calm waited for love-in-idleness, the flower touched by cupid's bolt and purpled by the poison of love. Oberon ordered Puck to fetch the flower, to squeeze it over the eyelids of the sleeping Titania. Proud Titania! Would she come around?

Shruti slipped out of her seat. She wanted to be closer to the stage when Titania came on. As she moved, the bloodshot letters of **EXIT** grew bigger, staring at her in the dark.

In this strange hall, to get closer to the play, you had to walk farther away from it. The round stage had no wings, no tapering tunnels of darkness through which backstage boys could peep into the stage. The stage rose from the carved crater at the beginning of scenes with the actors caught in still life. Sometimes they walked in through the vomitorium, the two exit trails between the rows that cut an axis through the circular hall.

Shruti looked out. A sickly yellow light gleamed in the corridor. Two ushers, dark, shrunken old men, sat huddled near the ticket cubicle, dozing off on each other's shoulders. The wan yellow light told a story: of a live playhouse that had gathered the dust of memory.

On stage the lovers sang the story of their star-crossed lives.

There were just a handful of brown heads, sleepy in the hall's thickening darkness. Behind the audience, rays of light and sound danced from a cubicle with a dusty glass front, throwing images on the walls around them, creating a noisy puppet show.

Swiftly Titania passed Shruti, her bare feet hushing across the hollow wooden plank of the threshold where the vomitorium opened into the corridor. She walked the narrow trail between two rows of seats and stepped onto the stage. She had a tiny crown of violet flowers on her head.

Happiness was a warm flood in Shruti's chest. This was the woman she knew. Touchable, through the sheen of makeup on her face, the tiara of the forest queen on her head. A woman who stepped into the angry whirl of silence. They pelted each other with curses like harried strings on a sitar. The king and the queen of the woods.

They fought over the little changeling boy they both loved and longed for, the boy all the way from the spiced air of India, fighting, forswearing each other's bed and company.

Shruti stood next to the vomitorium, a hushed body. From here, she couldn't see the whole stage, but a carved slice of it, like a crescent of the moon. The rest was hidden by the slope of the audience gallery on both sides. The stage looked angular and fragmented, a shadow cast over the lives that danced there.

It was the path through which they entered the story, sometimes flinging dead cigarette butts and chewed pulp of betel leaves on the way.

The knot deepened in the woods. Quickly it lost itself in the mist cast by Puck, its very own spirit.

22

Ahin took a deep breath. The narrow passage outside the hall smelled of tiny, crammed factories. Of glue and gunpowder.

Meera. She had walked a long way to find him.

She stood back, tried to melt into the sloping walls that flanked the vomitorium. A clumsy plank of wood hid part of her from Ahin. But he could still see her; he knew too well the sickly hue of lights cast off the stage. Most of her body was muffled by a fluid kurta. But the soft glow of the moonlit forest revealed dark jeans that hugged shapely legs like skin, one sharp knee pointing out, shoes melted into the darkness of the wood.

She stirred from behind the crested plank, glanced at him. There was no trace of recognition. She didn't remember. She had not really seen him during the few fateful seconds on Dhakuria station. It had just been a brief moment several days ago.

Tiny jets of air shot out from small fans tucked away under the audience gallery. They whooshed up from under her loose kurta, raising tiny whirlwinds. Rebellion tingled in Ahin's palm. The rebellious need to slip under that kurta, touch the smooth and cold skin of her arched back, encircle the concave hollow of her belly. The belly that could talk, chat, gossip. Grin and grimace. Cry and spit at you.

He crept closer to her.

"Where do you want to go?" he asked.

The fragrance of her body swam into his brain. A rare kind of fragrance, the dust of the outdoors and the faintest sour sharp sweetness, and was that a dry whiff of cigarette smoke?

"Just the way to the greenroom," she said, glancing at him sharply. "I need to talk to my aunt."

"Your aunt? Who?"

"Titania." She pointed to the narrow strip of light, where the queen of the woods was speaking to her elves in a voice bruised by longing.

"Garima?" he whispered. "Come with me. I'll take you to the greenroom."

Wordlessly she followed him. He knew she would.

They went around the hall to get to the stairs. Stairs that dipped into the pit under the stage. They tiptoed over trembling wooden planks that revealed pale light through cracks in between. The wood shivered under their feet. The hollow sound was drowned by the yearning music from the Athenian forest.

They stepped into a narrow passage where the air was warm and breathless. The greenrooms were across it, on the other side.

A rumble shook the stairs. Like a polite earthquake. Standing on the edge of the stairs, they saw the moon-drenched Athenian wood descend slowly, fill out the pit under the hall. A drugged queen stood among the gaudy streamers and shiny creepers, surrounded by fairies and a clown with a donkey's head, all frozen under a spell.

"That's a hydraulic piston," Ahin whispered in her ears, breathing warmly on her shoulders. "Floats on oil. Sucks the stage down whenever the scene needs to change."

As the stage sank into the crater, the clown took off his donkey head and lit a cigarette. The dry odour of burning tobacco filled the basement. Titania, too, took off her tiara of flowers. But she could not step out of the dream of midsummer.

They shifted the orchids and creepers around while the yearning music of violins filled the darkened theatre upstairs.

Two figures hid in the darkness while the stage changed to Oberon's wandering grounds, and fairies cursed and smoked and wiped their sweat.

The violin softened to a whisper. Oberon and Puck climbed back on the stage. Slowly it drifted upward, climbing the shiny hydraulic piston. The scene had changed on stage.

The basement was left empty. Without the moonlight of the drifting stage, it was only half visible, under the wan glow of a weak electric bulb.

They stepped out of the dark and walked into the basement. In one corner was a bed, curvaceous with soft plump pillows, covered with a homely bedcover. The bedposts had plastic flowers entwined around them. Flowers that were clean and well dusted. But crushed cigarette butts were everywhere. Wires and cables—red, yellow, green, and naked—tangled together in a witch's hair knot.

On the other side of the basement, there was a small wicker fence. It sat on a patch of plastic grass, through which a wooden toy tree had sprouted to life. A toy tree with painted leaves. Its shadow fell on a brightly lit stall of clay figurines.

It was the fragment of a fair.

Ahin whispered, pointing a finger upward. "Now we are right under the stage!"

The verses cut through the wooden planks of the stage, echoing in the room like the cries of strangled men and women.

"Peaseblossom," she spoke, her ears strung to the fleet-footed dance over the ceiling. "Cobweb, Moth, Mustardseed. The fairies are tending to Bottom."

"Have you ever acted in a play?"

Lightly she shook her head. *No.* She'd never acted in anything.

In the space cramped by discarded billboards and pyramids of bricks, his body breathed hers again. The sour sweetness of her fragrance whirled in his brain, the faintest whiff of cigarettes. Cigarettes? Cigarettes she had smoked, or smoke that had wrapped around her body during an evening embrace?

"You're a whore. The loveliest whore there was." Sharply, she turned toward him, her face mangled by disgust. "*Imagine.* Now repeat after me." Lovingly, Ahin smiled. "You want to play with me in front of my son?"

"What?" Disgusted, her face had a steely beauty. Beauty that could rip through your flesh.

"Let him stay?" Heroically Ahin offered her lines from memory.

"*Who are you?*" she hissed. Warm breath and the whiff of cigarettes singed Ahin. Slowly the world began to melt.

Inside him, the stage started churning. "So that he can listen to the radio while we fuck? Is that what you wish?" Like windswept candles, the lights grew frantic. "Now, repeat slowly . . ."

"Get away from me." Suddenly she was cold. Colder than she could possibly be. "Get the hell away!"

She shot out of the basement, groped her way to the stairs, stopping short for a moment before the darkness of the landing and its pile of junked furniture. A dark jungle with sharp edges and deep craters.

Over their head, horns and trombones shrieked. The city had finally entered the woods.

Ahin took a few steps toward her. Steps that drowned deep under the dance of a thousand elves above, a thousand light toes kissing the aged wooden planks of the stage. Magic and reality had made their peace. Swiftly he picked up a heavy iron photo frame, powdery with rust.

Helena loved Demetrius. Hermia loved Lysander. The lads loved the ladies back.

Mrinmoy, too, loved Meera. Loved her with a passion that bled. Blinded by love, he came up from the darkness that had swallowed the stage. Came up behind Meera.

Sharply he hit her on the back of her head with the jagged end of the frame. She fell in a heap on the furniture. He could not tell if she had shrieked—music and dancing feet thundered above and echoed wildly in the basement. He crouched over her crumpled body, inhaled her fragrance, fruity and smoky and drowned by the reek of dust and mold thick in the mangled pile of junked furniture. He whispered in her ears, "You have acted before, haven't you?"

A faint shiver ran through her body, the way the furniture shivered when a rat burrowed through it.

He touched her shoulders. "What you are," he whispered, "you have no idea."

He slipped his arms under hers and lifted her wilted body. "Take off your shirt," he said. Her head drooped to her left, and she trembled. But she did not speak. "You can't be shy with me!" He whispered. "Not with *me*."

He tried to prop her up but she wilted back again. He slipped his hands around her shoulders and unbuttoned her kurta. Gently he held her up, pulled her kurta over her head, and unclasped her bra. Smooth and bare, she fell back on him again, but the wan light under the stage barely reached this corner, and he could not see her well.

She was lean, and light in his arms. He picked her up and laid her on the bed in the corner of the basement where weak yellow light fell on the soft pillows, the curved plastic flowers, the soft and slippery stomach above her blue jeans. He sat on the edge of the bed. "A lovely complexion," he said happily. "You will glow in the spotlight."

Her skin glowed even in the watery light of the basement. Brown and smooth, a sculpted goddess yet to be clothed. With his fingers, he ran tiny circles on her body. Across her neck and her chiseled shoulders, breasts that heaved up and down with her breath. On her skin, his fingers traced blood, slow, dark drops that oozed from her hair. Hair that was Meera's bitter enemy, the hair that drugged her lovers and pulled them to her.

Gently he caressed her nipples to life. She had walked a very long way to find him. *Dusk* was now real. He felt hardness rise in his loins. *Meera.* The loveliest whore to ever walk on stage. To give pleasure to men. To cast a spell on them, on the eager eyes awake in the darkness of the audience gallery. He caressed her skin with the delight of a child, smearing it with the fine trickle of blood that oozed from her hair. Her eyes shivered and softly she gazed at him in a mute and lidless way.

His heart leaped. "The deer's greatest enemy is her own flesh," he said, breathing each word with care. "It is for her flesh that they hunt her down." His fingers ran circles on her stomach, slid into the tiny crater of her belly button. "Your body holds the seeds of your death."

Swiftly he dug into a cabinet under the bed, brought out a blue sari. A vibrant, shocking blue, like a peacock's neck, that gleamed even in the wan light of the basement. "Here," he said. "Put this on. It will glow on your skin."

Her lips shivered again. She was trying to speak. But she said nothing. A large teardrop slid down her cheek. Leaning closer, he saw her hair clogged with blood.

"Come," he said, turning her around, slipping the sari over her. "Put it on."

But she fell to the floor the moment he stood her up. She did not want to act.

Anger streaked through the dark. A purple anger. It flashed before his eyes for a millisecond, searing through the shadowy yellow of the basement.

"Just this sari," he said. "And then you breathe the character. You can. *You can.*"

She groaned. It was an ugly sound. She would not hold the sari. She did not care for her character.

The world began to crack. Into a million wriggling pieces. In his nostrils, Mrinmoy smelt the acrid odour of heat.

Holding his breath, he slid his right arm around her neck. Crablike, it trapped a soft, long neck. The sari fell from her body, lay in a heap around her legs.

"Have you been smoking cigarattes?" Mrinmoy asked lovingly. "Or sucking the smoke from a lover's mouth?"

He squeezed her neck dry. Veins, green and bloated, stretched from the back of his wrist to his elbow. But Mrinmoy was kind. He would not breathe while she suffered, the love of his life. The greatest actress who had ever lived.

In a house of pleasure.

A moan rang out from Meera's throat like a snake's tongue. It seared Mrinmoy's ears, dying in the room under the happy festivities that crowned Athens above. The sound died as her breath began to leave her.

As her body softened its struggle, Mrinmoy sought the fluid language of her stomach. The language of love and revenge and gossip that Meera used in bed, all through *Dusk*, through the navel left bare under a simple cotton sari, early in the twilight hour. Slipping his left hand around her, Mrinmoy buried his callused fingers in the smooth hollow of Meera's stomach, the deep hole of her navel. The navel that stared at you in bed. Smiled. Winked. Mocked you.

At long last, she was free of a life of sin. Her shapeless body wilted in his arms.

Carrying her to a corner of the bed, Mrinmoy laid her down, right under the plastic flowers. Kneeling behind her, he braided her hair into a rich, thick plait. Lovingly, he tied it around her neck, a hangman's noose.

Overhead, the stage drifted down, a brightly lit forest with a tangle of painted creepers.

On it stood Puck the trapeze artist. Slowly he filled the basement with song.

23

That night was all a dream. He ached to wake up but could not. The fleeting buzz of the doorbell and the knot of people outside the door, the police, neighbours craning their heads to see out of their windows, like birds stirred out of sleep. He sat on the bed in Mummum's room and stared at the door where the whispers clustered, but he couldn't rouse himself to walk toward the voices.

The silent group had fleetingly pressed the bell, as if ashamed to disturb the house. They were men of peace who spoke in hushed voices. Ori recognized Trinankur and his cronies—the muscular Pilot, Dushtu, and Tatai, men who made him shrink and hide on the streets. There were other men with them, whose faces he did not recognize. Peaceful, silent men whose eyes refused to meet those of the people in the house.

Their voices sounded hoarse when they asked for Rupa. But Rupa had appeared at the door almost before they said her name. *Rupa-Boudi.* Someone whom even the rowdy boys of the para were a little afraid of. Their voices dropped further as Rupa came to the door. Ori could not hear what was said. But he heard his father stumble his way to the door, speak in a mangled voice. Gently Rupa hushed him and led him away to his bedroom, put him to bed, as if he was a little boy with a fever. Shutting his door, she came back to the knot of men outside. This time Ori heard louder voices, and words that sent lightning streaks through his brain. *But he knew.* He knew where Shruti had gone tonight.

Rupa slipped back to her room and came out with her purse. She wrapped the anchal of her sari around her, slipped on her shoes, and was gone again without a word to anyone in the house.

Ori held his breath. Mummum's light snores floated through the gauzy screen of the mosquito net over her bed. He left the bed and walked into his parents' bedroom. He groped the pockets of his father's shirt draped around the hanger and filled his palm with coins. He would need bus fare. Slipping out of the door like an insect, he paused downstairs for a few seconds. The police car turned toward the main road.

He walked to the main road as fast as he could. He was already out of breath when he jumped into a bus that had slowed down to pick up passengers.

The theatre was at the heart of a strange carnival. A growing knot of people had gathered around it. A police car was parked at an odd angle off the pavement, as if it had crashed there. Wan yellow lights lit up the facade of the building where paint and plaster had peeled off to reveal a deep scar.

Two police constables stood at the door, blocking access. Ori slipped into the narrow alley that ran past the theatre. There was a small door at the back, thick with cobwebs. It creaked as he pushed through it. He stepped into the narrow passage around the circular auditorium. He paused at the sound of footsteps ahead, the brisk, heavy tread of police boots. But he had the confidence of a burrowing animal; he knew the tunneled passages better than the policemen and could melt into the darkness any time he wished. Swiftly he slithered through the play of light and dark to one of the heavy doors that opened into the auditorium. He peered into an empty and brightly lit hall, the gallery of seats like a tiny, deserted stadium around the circular stage, next to which stood a small knot of people ranting at each other. Suddenly he felt very small, powerless. He ached desperately to shake the building, toss and turn it around so that everything hidden came tumbling out. But he did not want to be spotted. Noiselessly he shut the door, and slipped back into the semidarkness of the passage.

He shivered. The theatre seemed to swirl around him. Inside him. Just the way he had seen the stage revolve.

Swallowing a few times to overcome the feeling, he moved slowly toward the cavern that led to the stairs. A strange mix of voices came from down below. Low, sharp whispers punctuated by loud shrieks. He thought he heard a voice he knew. He went down, groping his way in the dark, turning left on the landing to enter into a tiny cubicle that was dark and empty. The men's greenroom. He remembered it well. It was a place of laughter and gossip back when he was little.

He peered through the window above one of the tables. He could look down at the area around the foot of the stairs, at the knot of restless people illuminated in the bright light. Policemen in black and white. People whispered and shouted at the same time.

He wanted to rush down there but his legs would not move.

Heavy footsteps creaked down the stairs. He huddled in the dark and held his breath. As soon as the sound died away, he ran up the stairs.

Screams beat down on the walls of the theatre. A couple of men rushed past but they didn't see him. What was going on? Had people crashed through the main door? Had they beat down the constables? Ori stood for a moment, not knowing what to do. Then he found his way to the small door at the back and slipped out of the theatre.

Out on the streets, a small crowd foamed in brute anger. Ori moved away furtively, skirting the crowd. Brickbats came crashing down on the theatre, chipping paint and cement off its facade, smashing a ticket window and a light bulb. *The police should shut these places down*, someone shrieked. *Dens of violence and obscenity.*

A middle-aged man stood out in the crowd. He was tall and heavy and pale, clad in a cream-silken kurta, with sparse hair beautifully slicked down over his head. A princeling softened by a life of pleasure, a figure from old films. Quietly he was staring at the facade of the theatre. Then without a warning, he picked up a brickbat and flung it at the building. "Bring it down!" he thundered. "A smudge of filth on a clean neighbourhood!"

The brickbat bounced off the wall and shuddered its way back to the pavement. Ori looked back; fleetingly he felt he saw the theatre waver, sway tipsily. Would it fall and smash? He felt dizzy. He had moved away without realizing it, and stood behind a tree with a stone seat carved around its trunk. Four men sat on the seat, talking, shouting, gasping.

Ori wanted to shriek and call them. *Tell me!* But his throat felt dry. He couldn't speak.

It took him forever to reach around the gnarled trunk of the tree, touch one of the men. "What happened?" His voice trembled with fear. "Why are they shouting?"

The men turned to him.

"Go home, Baba," said the man. "Too late for you to be out."

"Why are there so many policemen?" Ori asked anxiously.

"Go home, boy!" one of the men stood up and thundered.

"Why?" Unmoving, Ori pointed to the theatre. "What's happened in there?"

"They found a dead body," the third man said without looking back. "Some actress."

The man's voice smeared crushed ice on Ori's skin. He shivered, and the road and the theatre and the crowd rocked and swayed again. He shot into the crowd, scanning the faces. Nobody seemed to notice him. He meandered back to the small door at the back of the playhouse but it was now knotted with people.

He ran back to the front, running straight into Abir, Tatai, and Dushtu. Tatai gasped. "Why are you here?" he thundered. But Ori barely heard him.

He stared at Abir. Abir said nothing. He didn't look shocked to see Ori. His eyes were glazed. He stared back at Ori.

"Go to bed," he croaked, "little boy. Go to bed."

〜〜〜

Ori threw up against the tree trunk. His innards screamed to come out with the flood of vomit. He leaned against the gnarled shoot that hung to the ground. He doddered again. He wanted to lie down in the viscous, brown-yellow pool.

His throat screeched with pain. He had pushed too hard. The pain burnt the inside of his mouth, the acid coating the lining of his throat.

He steadied himself. The strangest of questions shot through his head.

Strangled with her own plaits? How could that be? Shruti never braided her hair, hardly ever even tied it.

〜〜〜

In the wee hours of the morning, The Pantheon stood alone, unhurt except for a few brickbatted dents and one broken window at the ticket counter. The mob had vanished and the badly parked police car was gone. A dog whimpered in the distance.

Ori sat with the three men on the steps of the theatre, the nerves of his body dead and dry.

"Get a grip! You think he was the only one . . . driven to madness?" Tatai's voice cut through the dog's whimper.

It was a voice hoarse with fatigue. "Madness runs in his family. Madness over these theatre halls." He pointed to the ghostly structure of the theatre behind him.

"His brother was crazier. Crazier and craftier. A million times over. Whatever was left of their estates, he poured into that fancy revolving theatre. And his father blew the family jewels on an actress who romped through the north Calcutta playhouses back in those days. Set her up in a flat in Ballygunge. Watched her on stage and screwed her in the flat. And then watched her again the next evening."

Abir was silent. His eyes still looked glazed over.

"These theatres are built on ancient muck," Dushtu hissed. "You walk through muck to get to some of these playhouses."

Blood heat rose through Ori's skin. He closed his eyes and saw a throbbing, purple glow.

"It is time." Tatai's voice fell to a whisper. "We clean up this neighbourhood."

Abir stirred in the dark.

"It is time," Tatai whispered again.

24

"She was gone a long time ago," Rupa said, her lips not moving at all, her red-rimmed eyes staring at the wall. "The day whoring entered this family. She was no flesh of mine, not this girl." Her voice quivered with a strange affection. Her sister had grabbed her by her shoulders, shaken her frantically.

"Not since the day she started glossing her lips just like that slut. Just like her."

Rupa's words made him shiver. They scurried through his flesh like a scaly reptile. Fluently, Rupa cursed her dead daughter. Her stupid, stupid daughter who couldn't take her eyes off her aunt dressing up to go prancing on the stage before salivating lights. Deep into the night. Her dumb daughter who had followed her aunt to the dark pits of playhouses.

They had found her daughter naked, with the braid of her hair wound around her neck.

"She died a slut's death," softly she had whispered. Shivering, her sister had stepped away.

"A slut's death." Rupa's body shook feverishly.

But Shruti had not followed her aunt to that playhouse. Rupa would never find that out.

Ori had sent her there. But nobody would ever know. He could not talk. It would stay hidden.

As he turned to run, his skin was softly scratched by shapely nails. Unpainted, wind-encrusted nails.

What are you, crazy? Running away like that?
Slow down, nutcase! Wait for me.

※

Ori did not go back to the dusty, lime-green house in Dhakuria. The police and the Party wove a mesh impossible to claw through, walk freely, see daylight. Days and nights were a blinding blur spent in the poorly lit rooms of police stations and the offices of the Party, drizzled with endless questions. Tatai and Dushtu hovered over him, warm, hawk-like friends. For days he lived on the street snacks and soda they got for him, changed into T-shirts and pants a year too old that hugged him too tightly, for everything in the old house had grown smaller, a little moldier.

The narrow lanes squeezed down on him. He walked through them quickly, the sludge of fear heavy in his legs. The fear of a girl in a seaweed-green kurta. Dark green that blinded your eyes.

Months went by but he told them nothing. Nothing of what Shruti had whispered to him that afternoon in the bright, lime-green house. None of what he had whispered back. Nobody knew she had come to see him that day. That she had waited for his mother.

But for what he had whispered to her that afternoon, she would still be here, breathing hard on him, wrenching his arms, pushing him down to the floor, twisting him around till he did what she wanted. Laughing and cursing, spitting out dead blobs of chewing gum.

As he looked up, a flash seared through his eyes. A sliver of silver. The wisp of a watch across the thin, bony wrist of a girl.

He struggled to walk.

25

Slipping back to a life left behind, he trudged through the rest of Class Seven. There was no bitter court conflict, none of the urgent questions that made up an old nightmare. *Who did he love more? With whom would he like to live?* For years he had dreaded that question. He dreaded having to answer it in court, from the wooden enclosure next to a judge while struggling to gather his words.

Rupa had made up her mind. She would not let Ori's father rest till he found his way out. She would come home from work and head straight for their lawyer's home office a couple of houses away, every evening for months and months till all legal knots were cleared. She took apart everything Ori's parents had ever owned together, every single bank document, rummaged through the letters and diaries that she could find, and quizzed Ori about his mother with a sharpness that made him feel brittle inside. Sometimes during these visits to the attorney she took Ori's father along. His father now depended on her for everything, from getting his trousers pressed to giving the right answers to his attorney's questions. After a stormy fifteen years with a beautiful wife, he had wilted into a creature who felt safe and happy only with his plain and efficient older sister-in-law. *His Boudi.* His whole world.

Smoothly the lawyers plucked Ori free of his mother, a woman who could not support her child, a struggling actress who would struggle forever. Everybody saw that her desperate clutch was fueled by her neurosis, the same neurosis that broke and splintered everything that entered her life. A raving, destructive woman to whom you could not leave a thirteen-year-old boy.

Divorce. Some people pronounced it die-vorce, stretching the word with a shattering sound. Of things breaking.

A year went by in that unnameable state but at the end of it Ori escaped the court. His parents ended their marriage on stamp paper, paper that looked like banknotes, with the face of Gandhi and the Ashok Chakra. Truthfully.

Peace returned to Mummum's windblown looks. A bereft kind of a peace. She seemed to gather the reins of the house once more but, somewhere, Ori sensed that she was playing a part she didn't care for anymore. Suddenly you realized how old she was. Often she sat in silence, nothing on her hands but time. Great, empty chunks of it.

Meanwhile the truth trickled out, seeping through closed doors like blood from an invisible act of violence, on the wings of wind that blew in gusts through the house, carrying bad breath from room to room, through ancient, porous walls. But no one cared anymore.

>᠁<

Beyond the dense undergrowth of the para, he struggled to keep his home life a secret. But the nothingness stood out, especially when he walked out of school at the end of the day and went home alone. He didn't want anybody to know that he wasn't going back home to the old house, that home was no longer where it used to be. That these days, Dushtu and Tatai felt more like home than his parents did, scattered in different corners of the city.

He devised games to evade the homeward-bound crowd. All he had to do was to wait out the first half hour or so to make sure most of the parents had cleared out with their boys. Give it another fifteen minutes, and the school compound was an empty patch blazing in the afternoon sun, with nothing to show for the stampede that had gone before but a stray ice cream wrapper, torn pages from notebooks, some with algebra equations scribbled over them, vanished like they'd never been there. All he had to do during this time was to slip into one of the empty classrooms and read a book.

That afternoon, a strange story waited to be read and reread in his satchel, from a book snagged by accident at the school library.

Little Herr Friedman. As he read, a life tinier by two years tugged at him. He had slipped into the Class Five classroom, a room a little like a toy house with memories of fights and seat shuffles and its bitterness over quiz contests. He fought the drug of the past locked in that small toylike room, and pushed his mind back into the moist prose of the story. The quiet whirlpool of words in which his body, once caught, would dizzy around in sweet, sickening circles, till the rude bellows of Calcutta traffic startled him out of it. The story of the saintlike midget whose passion is awakened by a wild swan of the woman, the magistrate's wife. She would give him something no woman ever had. An untamed scent.

A human form darkened the sunlight falling through the door.

"Oritro," Miss Miranda asked, "what *are* you doing here? Why haven't you gone home?"

Waves of terror swamped his body, a muddy whirlpool churning his lower abdomen and groins. "I was . . . just . . ." he stammered, caught in the tug-of-war of fear and the truth, ". . . reading."

Miss Miranda's silhouette overcast the doorway; softly, she entered the classroom. Ori was already on his feet, his body rigid and ramrod straight.

She walked up to the desk he had left two years back. Clickety-click clickety-click went her heels, echoing deeper in the empty room. Long dark heel beats sparked off the walls, climbing the windowsills. Her deep maroon form towered over his croaking thirteen-year-old self, recoiling in horror at the splotches of dirt on his white shirt, shaped like a honey-combed ball of solid rubber, hair still plastered to the scalp with sweat. Savage patches of sweat on the white square of the shirt that the reading of no book could create.

"Look at you!" Her lips curled in the distaste reserved for poor spelling. "What a mess." He shrunk under the fearful authority of light perfume, sweetness with an acrid edge.

"Why haven't you gone home, Oritro? What's going on?"

He had to tell her. It was a billowy feeling in his belly, a soft rumble that signaled the need to go peepee. He was special, and she knew it.

"I go home alone these days, ma'am. Father O'Flaherty has given permission."

A frown appeared on Miss Miranda's forehead, curling up in the shape of a question mark. A cloudburst of shame warmed his mind.

"Alone?" The muscles of her long neck tautened as she spoke. "But why are you sitting here? Now?"

"I hate walking through there, ma'am. Alone." He would tell her everything. How it felt. "All the parents asking me questions."

"Questions?" He could tell from the tone of her voice that she knew the questions. "What questions?" She pushed further, hoping that she could will them away.

"Questions I don't want to answer." Under her looming fragrance he felt breathless, that sweet mist with an acrid metallic tip. She was *the school*, all of it, the school with a long brown neck beaded with faint drops of sweat on the skin. "Why my parents never come to school anymore. If I'm eating lunch properly." He scraped shame off his skin, bare and naked, for her to see. "I hate walking through there, ma'am. With all the parents taking the boys home. I hate walking alone with them around me."

Trying hard, and harder still, he had failed. To keep the swelling tear from gathering in the corner of his eye, to keep his voice from thickening. Long fingers and shapely nails touched his hair. He raised his head and her palm, curving against it, travelled with the movement, came to rest on his cheek, the dust-bitten cheeks about to be wetted by shameful tears.

"Never mind what they say, Oritro." Her palm waited on his cheek, warm skin breathing into his own, all the way to the upper curve of his neck. "Never mind."

Her smell was a blade that ripped through him. The tears came not only from his eyes but from every corner of his body, from every pore of his skin. The world melted and swirled, became an errant flood.

Suddenly Miss Miranda wasn't the school anymore. She reached out and hugged him. Her arms were long and brown and giving.

He cried. *And cried.*

For the first time in his thirteen-year-old life, he didn't try to hold back.

He had never imagined the sharp, shooting pain. Of the final, lasting separation of things—furniture, clothes' hangers, blankets, and lamps. Hungry stares and hushed voices in the para lanes. Fatigue on a face once beloved, now hated with searing anger. Anger which seared your inner organs. Drained of shame, he lost his face again. To her neck. To the skin above the neckline of her top, moist and alive. Warm in the nippy winter afternoon, felt through the mangled words he couldn't stop murmuring to her neck. Tasting the warm breath of salty skin through his words.

But he never let the ghost out. The dark ghost of a girl in a seaweed-green kurta. Of nails that scratched him faintly, pointy with accusation.

A ghost that clamped his throat shut and dried his tears.

Miss Miranda held him close. Cupping his cheeks in her palms, she stopped being a teacher. Forever.

Softly she kissed his forehead. Like a whisper. Let her lips linger on his skin for a second.

"Sit here and read as long you like." Her eyes darted to the door. "Leave whenever you feel like it."

Darkening the door again for a fraction of a second, her tall form vanished down the corridor. Above the teacher's table, the clock struck the hour. The clock on which some of them had learnt to tell the time, fighting the confusion of Roman numerals. I to XII.

Three o'clock and a bare school compound, swept clean of people. Even the sweepers were done for the day and were rolling their tobacco, getting ready to leave.

He thrust his book back into his satchel where it could hug the *Elements of Geometry*. Throwing the satchel across his back, he left the room. He stepped into the corridor, the long, bare stretch of woodcrafted green, comical against the gray pallor of classes IX, X, XI, and XII across the field. The coolness of the air hit him with a raw force of happiness. Nothing remained of the past, of the still air of the classroom left behind. He sprinted down the open stairs that led to the school grounds, his feet picking up the familiar rhythm on the wooden stairs on which some of them had learnt counting, one to eighteen. Clippety-cloppety-clop—one-two-three. Clippety-cloppety-clop— four-five-six. Eighteen was where numbers ended as there were no steps beyond that.

He counted his way down at a sprinter's pace. The school was empty. He felt invincible.

Eighteen steps and then to the left. He entered the passage that led to the outer compound, passing the assembly hall and the row of offices on his right. He didn't know that an empty school was so empowering, a spacious breath of beauty, drawn with crisp, clean lines.

The tall, flapping white-robed figure of Father O'Flaherty was coming toward him. The happy monk who could fly, perch himself on rooftops, and check everybody's hair for growth beyond Catholic-school rules. Closer and closer, three steps at a time, learning speedy math on stairless, level ground.

"How goes it, young man?" The tall priest paused next to Ori. "Have you been studying extra hard?"

"No, Father." He came to a breathless, smiling halt.

"Love school so much that you stay back past three?" Father was smiling too, and you could see that he didn't really want an answer. Just a smile to echo his playful mood.

He ran toward the gate.

Out on the streets, he took a deep breath of the mucky air and took brisk steps along the tram lines.

Abir would be waiting for him near his house at four.

26

As Ori walked into Pallabi's house, wickedness glittered in his heart like a precious stone.

It was a small room with a whole life cramped into it, most of it swallowed by a skinny bed, a little black-and-white TV next to a dressing mirror, and a clotheshorse with clothes neatly draped around its ribs. The neatness of poor people.

It was the room where Pallabi slept and cooked, edging the stove half outside the door to let the smoke out. Where she kept the ingredients for the makeup magic she cast on actresses, turned their hair into the shapes and textures needed on stage.

Where her five-year-old son, Rana, sat writing his letters and numbers, punctually at sundown, unwashed and unclean after muddy games through the rabbit warren of crowded rooms.

Tonight his mother would come back home late, very late. It was a big night for her. After years and years of shaping stage hairstyle, she was to step onto the stage herself. The moment she had waited for, all her life.

Ori took a deep breath as he smiled at Rana.

"Dada!" The boy's eyes lit up when he saw Ori. He moved aside his exercise book and stood up. "You? Here?"

Came to see what you're up to. Have you tried these? Nightmare by Cadbury.

Rana's eyes burned brighter. Nightmare, or Goodnight (as it said on the wrapper and on TV), it didn't make any difference to the boy still fighting his ABCs, who only cared for the glint of the silver wrapper, the nut-brown meat inside.

Nice, aren't they? Ori told Rana, his heart beating faster as he watched the boy listening to him with attention. They could go and get some more from North Point Confectioners on Central Avenue. How about it? Perhaps a bottle of Coke too, his very own bottle, to suck with two straws like last time. How about it?

Excitedly, they stepped into the slippery vein of the alley, an uneven stretch of red earth between the rows of tiny rooms. Ori wrapped an arm around Rana's thin shoulders. Suddenly he felt uncertain. The plan was as fragile as the boy's chicken-bone frame. He was crazy to put his hopes in it.

Abir wanted fire. He was childlike in the ferocity of his hatred. Pretty, pretty fires.

Walking through the forest of pavement stalls populated by shrieking hawkers, Ori didn't need to stop by a store to ask for shiny packets of Goodnight by Cadbury. The excitement of strolling the streets with Ori was quite enough for Rana. Quick and sure, Ori guided him in the right direction, his palm on the boy's back, a light touch of ownership.

After walking through the crowded streets for about fifteen minutes, the theatre hall loomed up before them, a heap of aged bricks dolled up with bright lights and a giant billboard. A giant billboard under yellow-white spotlights. It was abuzz with a swarm of seasonal insects and the tortured passion of the two women and the handsome, brutal man.

The Wishcar.

Starring Amar Nandi and Garima Basu

Play: Abhimanyu Goswami

Direction: Somnath Chattopadhyay

Inspired by A Streetcar Named Desire *by Tennessee Williams*

A title in Bengali poorly inspired. *Wishcar*? The source of inspiration was near invisible, the tiny letters hiding in shame under the paint-tormented faces of the three players. Of the three, Pallabi's face was the youngest and the most earnest. It was unknown enough for her name to be missing from the credits that might give pedestrians a pause before the hall. The Hairdresser's Dream. Fulfilled. Opening night.

The ancient theatre was dressed in gaudy lights and letters, just like the very first day Ori had found it, all by himself, four years ago, walking past women in shiny dresses, fire-red makeup on dark skin, and flowers wreathed around their hair.

He looked at Rana. It was opening night for this five-year-old too, an opening moment. A moment when there was nothing else for him except the unfamiliar face of his mother, five times its actual size, blown up and loud with gaudy paint, oppressed merely by thought. *Stella*. It wasn't for her to suffer. In this play, suffering was tenderly saved for another. But who would tell him that? He was blinded by the spotlight that shone on his mother's large, unhappy face on the poster, outshining the naked bulbs hanging over the paan-and-cigarette stalls scattered around the theatre.

In four years the place had changed only a little. There were people who would still swallow a small lump of fear before walking through this neighbourhood. A few more shops had sprouted over the years, but they were all of a slightly different hue, most of them draped with white evening bloomers, afloat in old Hindi film songs.

Rana couldn't take his eyes off his mother. Looking at him, Ori felt something sharp shoot through his chest. Yes. Rana *had* to watch this play!

"Come." He folded his palm around Rana's, warm and damp to the touch, and pulled at him lightly, unease darting through his body like a quick, slimy lizard. "It starts in ten minutes."

"But . . ." Rana stammered, still unable to take his eyes away from the lit-up billboard perched at the door. "Ma never takes me in. Children are not allowed!"

"Oh, come on! Don't you want to see your ma on stage?" He pulled at Rana's wrist, not too hard, not too gently. Rana wriggled behind him up the half flight of stairs that rose from the pavement, a small, wet animal.

They slipped into the hall. A murmuring silence hung in the air. They shot ahead like stray dogs that had found their way through a crack, winked at by the ushers who tore off part of their tickets and led them to the front row.

They were the most rotten seats, right at the corner of the first row, with a fine view of the steps that led up to the stage. They had to crane their necks to earn an angled view of the action.

The second bell went off just as they took their seats. Sharply cornered, Ori craned his neck, far back, left.

Quiet in the second row and closer to the aisle sat Abir, who craned his neck back to swap a sharp glance with Ori.

With the third bell, the auditorium darkened. An aching music strummed over the curtain, which wrinkled its way up. Time was when the third bell would stir a liquid fear at the pit of Ori's stomach. Today the third bell spread crushed ice over his fingertips. The ice of anxiety.

Unveiled, the stage revealed a world that lulled Ori into a familiar dream. Cheap yellow paint, plastered over the blistered walls of tiny homes cramped under jutting edges of slanting tiles, dirty-red things that could hurt your head if you didn't watch out. Railway tracks ran behind the tiny rooms that stood in a crowded heap. Once in a while, the sound of passing trains mingled with the whistle of ferry-boats afloat on the river just beyond the tracks. A poor para, if indeed it was a para, this ragged collection of tiled rooms by the tracks. But it was poverty touched by the fresh breeze from the river, the hymns and prayer songs wafting out of the riverside temples.

Two women sat chatting by the threshold of a house.

Two men walked past the tracks, toward the house, their once-white undershirts stained and sooty, wiry muscles angry with sweat. **Amar Nandi** led the way, the tireless, fearless cab-driver from dawn to dusk, occasional motor mechanic in the evening. A sinewy, demonic god, a pack of cards in his left hand, a bloodstained package in his right.

"Bipasha!" hollered the soot-sweaty god.

A pretty woman appeared in one of the doorways. A woman with delicate skin and voice, whose appearance next to the cowdung-caked walls was shocking and soothing at the same time.

And she looked beautiful. What had Pallabi done to herself? What magic had she worked on her hair, what miracle onto her skin?

"Must you shout?" The smooth-skinned woman raised her brows, a faint flicker that silenced the chatter of the two women sitting at the neighbouring doorway.

But not the soot-stained Amar, who just whistled, "Catch!"

"What?" Pallabi asked.

"Meat." He flung the word and the bloodstained package at her.

Shrieking, Pallabi spread her hands out, caught the package as it came crashing into her chest. The flight of the skinned chicken. Hugging the dead bird, she laughed, out of breath.

Chilled fingernails dug into the back of Ori's palm, splayed out on the armrest. To his right, Rana sat still, breathing fast, the fingers of his left palm clawing at Ori's—five cold snakes. The boy's body had stiffened.

After a few minutes, the fingernails slowly loosened and unhooked themselves from Ori's skin. Rana could not take his eyes off his mother, unrecognizable in her beauty, the alien look of her hair. He could not stop staring at the red-stained package she cradled like a baby in her arms.

Ori stole a quick glance at Abir at the other end of the second row. He was half hidden behind people, his features indistinct in the semidarkness. The nightmare had started too early. Too early.

"Are you okay?" he whispered to Rana.

The moment Pallabi left the stage, another woman wandered in. Her pale blue sari floated on the stage, keeping away from the touch of the dung-blessed doorsteps and women's underwear hung out to dry on the communal rope.

She was Teesta, Bipasha's elder sister, lost and confused in the maze of yellow rooms behind the railway tracks. A squeezed pip of a woman, walking wearily. Beauty shying away from the harsh light that might unmask the furrows of her age.

A role warmed to perfection for **Garima Basu.**

The sisters' union brought tears to the audience's eyes. In a flurry of laughter and gasps and sobs, they poured out their loves and nightmares to each other. The house of wealth that had nourished the sisters was gone. Sucked into the black hole of debts, leaving the gold-caressed Teesta a poor teacher in a primary school, a round-spectacled Didimoni who dressed in bright blue saris the texture of dreams, running from loud lights that might reveal the toll the violence of time had taken on her, lay bare the trail of disaster she had left in her wake.

She was still shaken by the sight of the yellow homes beside the railway tracks where her flesh-and-blood sister lived with a low-life cabdriver with whom she had eloped, escaping the dreary corridors where the marble had begun to wear out, the mahogany turning to dust.

But the night sucked her shock away and drowned her in cheap alcohol. Liquor-wet, Garima's body lost the sari anchal draped around it. Trailing in the dust, it revealed the form of a swan imprisoned in a black silk blouse to the reddened gaze of the four card players who had gathered to party at Mani's place that night. Garima stretched out, breathing the sourness of liquor into her sister's mouth, the arrogance of her blouse-clad chest rising and falling with her breath, swaying her body to jazz vocals on late-night radio, bathed in red light, aching for pain. Amar hated her. He loved nothing better than to make her suffer.

Fingernails dug into Ori's thigh, deep, very deep. His very own nails.

Staring at the trembling, proud-chested Garima on stage, Ori could smell the sweat on his own body. The salty, disgusting kind of sweat that filled you with nausea at the feel of your own flesh, your crawling skin. The joke was on him, and him alone.

He arched his neck to the left to catch Abir's piercing glance, now turned in their direction. He had leaned ahead, restless.

On stage, the next morning brought a well-meaning glow. Amar's room had vanished with the night. Quick-footed set boys had brought back the yellow cardboard facades of rooms by the railway tracks. There, the morning brought Amar, muscles rippling through a clean undershirt, walking up the stairs to the right with a red-stained package in his hand. Wet, heavy, and bloody. Right past the two boys in the remote corner of the audience.

Loudly, he called out to her again. As Pallabi came out with fresh annoyance on her face, Amar laughingly heaved the package toward her. Clutching at the air, she caught it, elbows clamping together in a loving kind of fear. Blood streaked her sari like a splash of Holi. Breathlessly, she laughed, and daylight shone over the railway tracks.

A muffled cry cut through the stupor that had cast its gauze net over Ori. Startled, he looked to Rana, now a rounded crab with a sunken head. His palms were clamped over his mouth in a wild reflex of horror that had escaped, muffled, through his bony fingers.

On stage, Pallabi smiled. A fine dew of sweat glistened on her upper lip, alive only to the front row. On the seat, the boy shivered in the throes of a malign fever.

Ori felt his head reel. What would happen to their crazy plan?

"Get real, Abir," Tatai had said, the street muscle who had aged into a peaceable pillar of society. "This is not the kind of hall that catches fire easily." Not this one. "Hatch a better idea."

But in this play, suffering was saved for someone else. A woman Ori knew and did not. On stage, the foulmouthed Amar hated Garima with a passion, for hiding a slippery past to play the round-spectacled schoolteacher. To lure in young boys with her aging snake eyes, lidless, unblinking.

"Tell me if I'm wrong, sister, saali of mine? How did you play with your fifteen-year-old student to lose your schoolteaching job? Where did you touch him to get the blood rushing to his cheeks?"

Heat rose in Ori's ears. His nostrils filled with a strange fleshy smell, roasted, fragrant flesh. It would be easy to slip out through the exit right next to them, slip out of the hall, shoot out far, far away from the theatre, through the thick aroma of white evening bloomers. Fourteen-year-old boys often did run rudely from the middle of shows.

Next to him, Rana fidgeted in his seat. He was at the end of his tether, and he wanted to go soo-soo, spray paint the wall with piss.

As the lights grew stronger on stage, Garima's face revealed deeper wrinkles, deeper ravages of time. The loss of a bejeweled past, and the fear of losing the youth that was long gone without her permission, gnawed at her. Why did Amar hate her so? The scene revealed the mystery. Liquor-wet, Garima drew inside the boy, the gangly, stuttering teenager who had knocked on the room's cardboard door one lonely afternoon when Amar and Pallabi were out. He was doing the rounds to raise money in that cardboard community for the Kali Puja around the corner, the festival of the demon-slashing, blood-drinking, the blackest goddess of the season. Wandering off from the rest of his friends, he had knocked on this door alone, drawing a rum-moist Garima to its threshold. No, she didn't have any money to spare for the night-sky fireworks, but would the young man have a lighter, a box of matches he could spare? He smoked, didn't he, the naughty boy, and these soft lips were ever so parched with the heat of tobacco, weren't they? But they still tasted sweet, didn't they?

Come here, I want to kiss you, just once, softly and sweetly on your mouth!

"Just once," she whispered.

It would be nice to keep you, but I've got to be good—and keep my hands off children.

Breathlessly Ori looked away from the stage. From the lilt of Garima's liquor-soaked words. A bright pain twisted inside his inner organs, like spring-coiled toys in the hands of cruel little boys.

Rana watched the stage with boredom heavy in his eyes and soo-soo heavy in his bladder, his feet kicking the air in front.

The play crawled to the final act. After another moonless night, Amar came up from the other end of the stage, climbing the stairs from the audience one more time. Before Ori and Rana, close to where they sat, stood Pallabi, an unborn child straining her belly, a life which stretched against her skin as she stooped to draw water from the tube well outside her room. But Amar was thoughtless, on his way back from the butcher's, newspaper-wrapped lump of dead flesh in his hand, his daily meat. The slow swagger of his entry brought the touch of cold skin on the back of Ori's arm. Cold and moist boy fingers crawled back, a crinkly spider with a dead soul. Amar whistled. *Here you go, baby. Make kebabs tonight?* The package flew across the stage, a red-stained lump arching through the riverside morning light. Heavy-bellied Pallabi swiveled around, about to fall on the sharp, blistered earth, crush her heavy, living belly against a jagged piece of red tile.

"Did Rana come to see the play with you?" she asked without turning around.

"Yes." His voice trembled. "He really wanted to see the play."

"He shouldn't have," he said quickly. "He wouldn't listen." The words, he worried suddenly, came too fast.

She said nothing. He wondered, suddenly, if the mirror had misted up before her face, obscuring the reflection of his face. Mirrors trapped you in the truth. They moistened if you sighed, and sometimes if you were angry.

"Abir was there too? I think I saw him there."

"Abir?" Swiftly, he killed the cold panic slithering through his voice. "Here? No. Why would he come here?" He looked around and ached to get out. The airless room stifled him. Stuffy and shiny, choked with clothes and lipstick and rouge and talcum powder. A room that wanted to smother and kill him quickly.

"Come closer." Did her voice soften, suddenly? "How's school? You didn't tell me."

He took baby steps again, closer to her. They met in the mirror again. He dreaded seeing the fine lines of age on her face, hidden by coarser wrinkles given by makeup. He had never seen her in a play, he felt, where she had to dress up to look like someone so much like herself.

"Keep away from bad company." Suddenly her voice was distant again.

He shivered a little.

"School is fine. I'm in Class Eight now." The words rushed out. "Rupa auntie irons my school uniform. And she packs my lunch box."

"Does she?" A strange blankness appeared in her eyes, as if the bright lights had suddenly left her blind.

"She makes lunch for Baba too." His eyes met hers in the mirror, and his voice tightened.

"Does she?" Her voice echoed in the shiny toy room. Lifelessly.

27

It started a month ago, that same night when the crowd battering down on The Pantheon had scattered and the shrieks had melted into silence. Slowly everyone had vanished into the dead hour. The smell of violence hung in the air like spent gunpowder.

"It is time," Tatai had whispered. "We clean up this neighbourhood."

Speech died on the steps of the theatre. For a long time. Silence thickened in the darkness.

"It is time," Tatai had whispered again, as if in a trance.

"We've tried," Dushtu said. "It's an old nasha in this city. Generations and generations of addicts, way too many nutcases."

"We need something," sharply Abir broke his silence, "that shakes the ground under their feet. Break a limb or two."

"Don't go there," Tatai had said coldly. "You don't know where these things lead to."

"But accidents happen, don't they?" Abir glanced sharply at Ori. "What about fire hazards?" Ori looked away, refusing to meet his eyes.

The others dismissed Abir quickly. It was but the fantasy of a man driven to derangement by the hunger for vengeance.

But over the next few weeks, the fantasy congealed slowly, took up a body. It could be fun, stirring up hell to take some shine off a theatre or two. Shaking up the theatre wallahs a bit. Giving them a taste of local anger, simmering in people sickened by the playhouses playing raunchy dances and cheesy music, shocked and silenced by a grotesque murder.

A glint shot through Dushtu's eyes. And a shiver ran through the muscled shoulders now softened by middle age. Quickly he killed the glint, washed his hands off the joke. Tatai laughed it off again. Abir was, after all, a college kid just pretending to be a badass. *Did he even know what these things could lead to?* Battle wounds, lost lives, years and years behind bars.

The two older men knew well the tangle of law and order, its cracks and crevices. They were Party members in charge of the para's peace and happiness, its public morality as beaten into shape in the crooked lanes and the tea shacks lining them.

They offered silence, silence that softened and mellowed with time. Silence that was support in an alien language that you dared not translate. Not to yourself, not to anyone else in the Party. Most definitely not to Trinankur, the Pretentious Party Pillar who acted as if dog turds on street corners soiled his image, and that of the Party. Who the hell did he think he was, their bloody daddy?

But the Party would not support such violence. They would not engineer arson even though they wanted the old playhouses of north Calcutta wiped away, the dark traces of decadence cleaned off the city skyline. They were too many in the Party who swore by theatre and wanted the new theatre to take deeper and deeper route in the city. The theatre of change and revolution.

The little group splintered off the Party, seethed in discontent. *Bloody Party!* What did they know? How could plays change the world?

"It's the press," Tatai grimaced. "Shit freezes in their guts at the look of newspapers."

"If they catch us they'll cremate our fathers and fourteen generations before them," Dushtu said. "If the press catches us, the Party will cut off our dicks."

"So we're on our own." Abir shrugged. "Big deal!"

They could not mess with fire, not even with the idea. Flush it out of your head! Arson was just the bad headlines of gaudy papers.

"So what do we do?" Abir asked gloomily. "Let the show go on?"

Gently Ori had spoken.

"Children are not allowed," he had said. "For many of these plays."

"Children?" Dushtu's whisper echoed the silent horror on the rest of the faces. Of course. What was he thinking? What sick mind dreamt of a child in this world? In the audience? In the powdery warmth of the greenroom?

"Children!" Ori went on, the moist breath of memory on the nape of his neck. "You can't have children in the hall. They shriek and cry and spoil everything."

Something changed in Abir's face. He leaned closer to Ori.

"Really?" he asked, his question a piercing arrow.

"Really." Slowly Ori's wandering gaze returned to Abir's eyes.

"They are a pain, the kids," Abir drawled slowly, swirling the words in his mouth. "Shrieking and pissing every few minutes. Don't care where they are."

"There are things they can't watch." Torture and suffering, the cabaret dance of near naked women, which brings down heavy adult fingers over young, blinking eyes like dark curtains. "Worse . . . worse . . ." Ori spoke, deep in a dream.

"What?" the three men whispered together, a hoarse chorus.

"Someone they love crying on stage."

Rana had crawled into his head right at the moment he'd heard that the time had come for Pallabi to shine on stage. He had stayed there, a tiny, lit-up puppet in the darkness of his mind. The hairdresser's little boy worshipped him, followed him around like a puppy. A woolly ball of shrieking panic. A skinny stick of dynamite.

It had worked like a dream. *Absurdly.*

Fear that had tried to smash the stage, had reached Dushtu and Tatai quickly that very evening. Stunned them! What? The shrieks had soured the play? Shocked the players? Scattered the audience? Right there? The theatre that hadn't paused its performance even on evenings when police raided the neighbourhood, raising a cordon of hell around the building. *That place?*

Suddenly they were gripped by an alien excitement they could not fight any longer. The two older men who had offered nothing but silence so far, a softened silence that you were not permitted to translate. It was excitement their bodies betrayed, sparking greed in their eyes. Could be fun indeed!

The fun would not stop. Over the next few months, every kind of theatre in the para was bullied breathlessly. No play could go smoothly in the halls and auditoriums dotting the crooked lanes. The few amateur clubs—low-budget affairs with wide gaping holes in their management—were fair game for any kind of vandalism. They were toy houses with scaffoldings of wicker and cardboard, frail electric wires easy to cut through, careless crews easy to confuse. Damaged sets, light trouble, property trouble, shows ran into a jagged terrain.

Sometimes even Tatai and Dushtu had to look away. From Ori and Abir and their scarring passion for shattering chandeliers and burning holes in the sets. Once in a while they caught Abir staring at Ori in the orange hue of the wings, watching every step of his. But Abir would return to himself quickly, trimming his mind into a deadly object, guided by the smell of glue and makeup like a beast of prey. Sometimes he leaned closer to Ori, whispered a joke and tried to laugh, but laughter never came.

Tatai and Dushtu provided information, knowledge about the habits of the police, the character of local boys roused by violence, the frayed nerves of local hawkers and the ploys of beggars who littered the pavement before playhouses. Sometimes they talked about the hidden frailties of impregnable padlocks and the toxic nature of certain kinds of stain removers. They hummed and buzzed around Abir and Ori, touching them with affection but not wanting to be seen with them in the light of day. Ori noticed nothing. He forgot thirst or hunger for days, sawing away at wooden boards and rusted locks, talking to new teenage recruits to their desultory gang.

Once in a while Dushtu's face would tighten with anxiety. He would whisper, ask them one evening to let things go. Not to mess with a troupe where someone had connections with the police or a politician. Ori would see through him like he was a man made of glass. Abir's face would grow grim, his voice tight; he would argue with Dushtu. He would start to shake, about to spin out of control. He was hotheaded and could be crazy when people tried to stop him.

It was easy to gather a few souls who bathed in violence, who lived to wreak havoc, on embattled college campuses, locked factory gates, the darkness of theatre halls, boys barely out of their teens who loved nothing better than to break locks and shatter glass. Tatai and Dushtu lent them the force of rightness they stole from the citizens' council, keeping the rest of the council dark about their complicity with a gang of vandals. The council would be shocked by the knowledge of its own fingers in the violence, and who knew what the Party would say?

※※※

Ori went and saw his mother from time to time. The court had ordered that he live with his father's family, as it was clear that his mother couldn't support him. Not financially, not emotionally, not with a life of routine and calm and clean crockery. She had visitation rights, which she never exercised; how could she walk into the old house again, through the web of crooked lanes left behind? It was almost as if she could see how Rupa had pulled Ori close to herself, making him her own. She knew that it was now Rupa who packed his lunch box and pressed his school uniform; she didn't know that Rupa now knew the names of his friends better than she had ever cared to know. Did she know that Rupa had forced Ori's father to go to the doctor for a checkup and that they had found things were all wrong with his heart? That Rupa, after much shrieking and pleading, had finally managed to train the old cook to prepare his father's meals separately? Did his mother know that Mummum had suddenly become very, very old, that she hardly left her room anymore? The questions whirred in his head like seasonal insects every time he went to see her, in the dusty clamour of rented rehearsal rooms, in the yellow light of greenrooms, in the windswept, lime-green house in Dhakuria.

His mother noticed little these days. Shruti's macabre death had dealt her a sharp blow, shaken up her relationship with the stage. Telltale signs of age, too, had also begun to creep up. The creases under her eyes and the gray streaks around her temples were, most of the time, shrouded by well-done hair and makeup, but their arrival had softened her faith in herself like a milk-caked sweet slowly going rancid, a shadow over its crisp whiteness. And her plays were shadowed by a curse of ill luck wherever she went, the ill luck of nasty, bitter accidents. The ill luck of rarely being able to finish a smooth performance.

"Still come to watch my plays, do you?" she would say to the reflection behind her when he came to see her in the greenroom. Nearing the end of Class Nine, he now stood a head taller than her seated form staring back at him in the mirror; sometimes she tilted her chin upward a little while speaking to him. The yellow light in the greenroom left a weak halo of the character she had just played on stage. Watery disbelief fought exhaustion in her voice, a steady draining of faith in her life on the stage and beyond it.

As she stared at him in the mirror, she reminded Ori of the dark theatres that were breaking off in flakes of plaster and cement, crumbling into dust. That was the world that had made and nourished her.

She was a playhouse with silver-streaked hair and skin beginning to wrinkle. A playhouse ready to vanish.

28

The strange, cracked-plaster grimace on the facade of The Pantheon drove a lump through Ori's throat. Thirteen months after that unreal night, the playhouse still felt like a dream. Nothing about it was touchable. Not its yellow walls, loud and bright in spite of the dust and chipped paint, not its windows like drowsy pigeonholes, not the winding flight of stairs that had crumbled on the pavement. Nothing was really there.

Next to him, Abir was a heavy, lumbering presence. Quiet. Very quiet. Only Dushtu leaped ahead, a restless man. His excitement made him look younger than his years, a springy excitement that fired up his limbs as he slipped into that winding, cavernlike house. They *had* to come with him. Now. What had he heard? He wouldn't say.

News of heart-chilling happiness.

"We are ready." His eyes had crinkled in a soft smile.

They walked through the meandering passage that circled the round auditorium, the three of them—Ori, Dushtu, and Abir. They trod lightly through the fading light of early evening that fell through undefined openings, glass panes, and half-shuttered windows. Walking along the passage that snaked around the circular auditorium, they caught glimpses of strange, tiny factories. A room groaning with the rusty music of welding machines and thick with the aroma of glue. A fragment of a printing press where they pressed and bound book covers. The crafting of firecrackers in a strip of the passage. Dark shirtless men toiled wordlessly, stuffing shiny rolls of paper with deep blue powder, sprinting against time to beat the deadline of Diwali, the grand night of firecrackers just a few days away.

They trod past the door to the auditorium. They walked all the way to the stairs and climbed up two flights, arriving at a place that looked like the old abandoned set of a play that had not been staged for many decades.

A veined iron gate, one that had shielded the passage from the world for decades, lay in a crumpled heap of rust on one side. It was guarded by a pair of cats who snarled angrily at the sight of strangers. Ancient framed posters of the long-dead Mani Mullick's plays shone gaudily on the walls. Was it a home that was part of a theatre? Or a theatre that was part of a home?

Grabbing hold of the rusted heap of the gate, Dushtu shook it hard.

"Nishith!" he called hoarsely. "Ei Nishith."

A man slipped through the door at the end of the passage, mild panic on his face.

"Dushtu." Relief danced on the man's face for a moment. It quickly vanished at the sight of Ori and Abir. "Who's with you?"

Nishith had once been a good-looking man. Short and pale and profusely hairy, he was now a knotty bear with a pleasant human face.

"Friends," Dushtu said with a soft smile.

"Friends?" Nishith's face was furrowed with doubt. Next to him, the large gray cat sat on the steps and fixed her stare on them. At that very moment, another man appeared behind Nishith, a colossal, pale-skinned man in a cream kurta and loose white pyjamas. He filled the passage with his generous girth and a voice moist with laughter. "Dushtu! Come in."

Ori remembered the face. Standing in the middle of the fuming crowd that evening, this man had hurled a heavy brickbat at the facade of this playhouse. "Bring it down," he had roared.

They walked into a large room, the sunlight of the large man's open affection drowning the cloud of Nishith's suspicion. From high above on the wall, the stuffed head of an antelope with winding horns stared down at them.

"The Party is catching them young these days!" The large man plopped down on an ornate, wooden armchair and slipped a melting smile to Ori. "Pretty young!" His brows danced. He was pale, the colour of a fine, well-kneaded ball of flour finished with a sweaty, perfumed shine. Ori, Dushtu, and Abir squeezed together on a cushion-littered cot, their elbows grating against one another. Nishith squatted on the floor next to the large man and looked at them warily.

"He's older than you think, Roy." Perched on the edge of the cot, Dushtu looked tired. "Not yet fifteen but far older than you can imagine."

"Ah." Roy's eyes smiled at Ori. "Look at those glasses!"

"Look here, Roy," Dushtu said. "The Party has tried to clean out these playhouses forever. Just spit and whistle and booze and violence. Whores jiggling their bellies on the stage while cabbies and truckers whistle from the audience."

Wordlessly, Roy took out an expensive-looking pack of cigarettes and passed it around. Abir and Dushtu each took one. Roy held the packet out to Ori, a liquid smile in his eyes. Ori raised his eyes and stared back, not touching the packet. "No?" Roy's smile deepened as he slipped the pack back into his pocket. He fished out a thin lighter and lit a sharp blue flame, a tiny piece of frozen lightning.

"We've roughed them up a bit too. Have to keep the para clean and sober." Dushtu leaned forward to light his cigarette, and pulled back, the tip red and glowing. "Wouldn't have been easy without Oritro." He looked at Ori through a wispy cloud of smoke. "He's not a child, Roy."

"What I've been telling you all along," Dushtu paused, suddenly breathless, "is that people, they're not going to care if something terrible happens to this place." He gestured below as he spoke, to the theatre that was part of the home. From the home that was part of the theatre.

"You are a leader of the local citizens' council. And a Party member." Roy began to rock slowly on the armchair, a big, happy baby. "And you know nothing of the tide of the times. The Pantheon is gone. What you have here is a dead shell. All of these theatre halls are gone. The whole song and dance. People don't give a fuck if you cremate a shell."

"Cremate?" Abir's voice sounded disembodied, a floating ripple of anxiety. He looked at Ori for a millisecond before averting his glance.

Ignoring Abir, Roy looked straight at Ori. "What if?" his eyes were frigid, unmoving. "These buildings catch fire easily. A tiny accident. Wiring gone berserk. The genius of human idiocy. Who'll notice the next day that it's gone?"

Silence thickened in the room.

"Nobody!" Roy said.

Not even the police. Not so much as to matter. Why would they? The Pantheon was a long, long way from the kind of theatre the Party cared about. This was the theatre of mercenaries, the stage of costly chandeliers and epic costumes. The kind of stage the Party would love to see go up in flames. Roy was certain, as certain as he was a Party member himself. So what if he was a land-grubbing building promoter, a man haunted by wealth as if it were his shadow? *How about another cigarette?* No? The Party had built its own halls, sleek, modern, fire-cautious buildings with Western-style lavatories where the drama of class struggle was played out daily with nothing but shadows on an empty stage. Hair-raising stuff that would change the world. Name a single person, barring the insurance companies, who stood to benefit from the prolonged life of these empty shells. Name just one!

"Bloody hawks too, these insurance people." Stretching on his armchair, Roy raised a silken rustle, the caress of his glossy shirt on his smooth, flabby arms. "They don't pay up easy. But that's your fight, Nishith. You've inherited this playhouse and all its sickness."

Nishith wasn't pleased at the mention of a fight. But Dushtu knew the people who'd insured this hall, and he could teach Nishith a few tricks that he could make the most of the prime cut of real estate that had fallen straight on his lap after his mad-dog uncle had been cuffed to safety. Roy was quiet. Finally. Laughter stirred like the ticklish feet of ants across Ori's chest, arms, and legs. His mind wandered as Dushtu broke down the basics of the perfect insurance claim. Ori didn't realize when, in the semidarkness of the room with the stuffed antelope staring down at them, he had slipped off the edge of the cushioned cot and wandered to the door.

Half awake, he stepped into the room next door, a large room of chipped marble and open windows through which dry, grating smoke floated in, from clay ovens freshly lit in the neighbouring slums. It was a room with alien contours, corners, edges, veins, and bones. The ceiling as high as an amphitheatre. A bed stood in the centre, a massive antique piece of rich, burnished wood that needed a ladder to climb into, its ornate posts fringing a mirror of cracked, faded glass. Overlooking the neighbouring slums were windows framed with carved wooden shutters as elaborate as the gates of fortresses. An alien room that looked strangely familiar. *Why?* Ori stood, wondering, before the sheaves of paper that crowded the tables, layered with a patina of dust undisturbed for months. His mind blanked out for a moment, and then returned to him again. They were scripts of plays.

Tangled voices rose and fell in the next room, fighting each other, falling into a smothered heap. Something about their urgency reminded Ori of the sound of rehearsals that used to fill his evenings, years and years ago, from adjoining rooms where he fought silent battles with homework as muffled storms rose and fell through the walls. Rented rooms by the roadside dented by the sound of passing cars. Today Roy's choric voice soothed and calmed the anxious Nishith, driven to panic by his sudden rights over the playhouse given to him by the violent insanity of Uncle Ahin. What was he to do with a dead shell of a theatre haunted by nothing but memories?

Ori wandered through the room while half his mind swam in the tangle of voices next door. Suddenly he realized that he was treading on tiptoes. Something about the room told him that it had not been touched for a long time. Shrouded in layers of dust, the room dared you to stir its long-dead life. Playbills and posters of plays produced over the years in The Pantheon and the neighbouring theatres lay scattered in the room, but with a kind of design that it took you a few minutes to figure out, like a stage set a little too cleverly for its audience.

Next door, Roy's sleepy voice cleared the fog that had greeted them on their arrival at the rusted gate. "I guess I have zamindari blood too, or else why would I dream of prime strips of land day and night? But Nishith's the real lucky one. He gets a couple of luxury flats out of this one, and a fortune to wheedle out of the insurance companies. Of course the bastards will pay. It's going to be the deadliest show they've ever paid for. A fire waiting to catch for years."

"Diwali night," Roy's voice drifted through the door. "Lots of fires that night. Firecrackers popping like crazy, fires shooting off everywhere."

"Diwali night," Dushtu repeated, as if in a trance. "The firecrackers will drown everything."

Ori heard the voices but they failed to touch his mind, which trotted across the room, gliding across posters of decades-old plays pinned and pasted across walls, mahogany cupboards, a clouded Belgian mirror. *Immortal Thorn*. The epic of a family scarred by history! Every Thursday, Saturday, and Sunday at Rangmahal. *The Emperor and the Belle*, forever and forever across the spine of the door, loud colours dulled by time and dust. *A hundred and fifty weeks to packed houses!* Never, ever to fall off the door, to be torn from the fine embrace of cobwebs. The cushioned lap of a large armchair held a bizarre mélange of objects. Several saris, some in loud colours, some quiet and homespun. Two store-bought jars of pickles, unopened. An empty pack of John Player King Size cigarettes. A bankroll of fresh, crisp fifty-rupee notes, a sheaf of scribbled papers photocopied many times over, strung together with black rubber bands and red ribbons. They were scripts of plays never printed. Ori was tempted to read them, but words in the faded ink of the photocopied sheets were hard to decipher.

The thin sheaf of papers that peeked out from under the pillow looked different.

Long sheets of brittle paper etched with writing in a beautifully flowing hand, the letters welded to one another in a riverine rhythm.

Lifting the pillow slightly, Ori pulled out the sheets, which threatened to break at his touch. The very first sheet was pockmarked at the top with a sprinkling of words in a hurried hand.

> *School got over at one forty in the afternoon. He walks out alone. White shirt, white pants. Green and gold tie. Gold and green belt. Into the dark passage under houses and offices. Kicks at dried dogs' turds like he's trying to score a goal.*

Shock was a cold, live animal in Ori's mouth, gasping up his throat, caught in a losing struggle with reddening shame. He kicked, didn't he? Everything in his path. Broken bits of earthen cups, stones, paper scrunched into balls, and dried dog shit? Shamefully he read a choppy, chuckling map of his trip from school to the fresh-painted emptiness of the house in the land of ploughed fields and naked railway tracks. Dodging his way through the forest of commuters at Sealdah South. Ticketless, into the hanging claws of the Canning Local 4:49. Swinging his water bottle all the way.

He turned the page. The title page was next. Large words at the heart of the page, in dark, faintly smudged ink.

Dusk. A Play in Three Acts. *By Ahin Mullick.*

Ori turned the page with effort. Large, heavy, and brittle pages, filmed with dust that felt powdery to the touch.

ACT I, SCENE I:
Twilight in a house of pleasure. Melody from old romantic Hindi films on the radio. Meera and Lila, the two women of the house, busy with their evening toilette, before carved mirrors lit up by bright lights. *Spotlights off.* Light fixed above the mirrors reflecting to the audience seated around the stage.

He read on. The rehearsing voices beyond the door were lost to him.

Time stopped. For twenty-seven minutes. Ori read fast. Very fast. With a heaving mind, despite the half-awake calls that came from the next room.

"Ori. *Ei*, Ori! Where are you?"

Slowly they became real. And then melted back again into unreality.

Mrinmoy gave Meera the loveliest gift of all. The gift of death. He loved her deeply enough to come up from behind and strangle her. *Spotlights to shrink and focus on their faces as Meera dies, the rest of the stage in the dark.*

After her dead form had crumpled to the floor like a wilted flower, Mrinmoy gave life back to the rich braid of her hair, tangled it around her neck, a silken chain wound several times over. A woman killed by her own beauty. *Curtains, the faintest of music, growing stronger, the song in Meera's voice from backstage.* The loveliest whore selling a fragrant dusk.

Lovingly, Mrinmoy had braided the corpse's hair, woven a rich plait. Wavy, like the curved edge of an ornate bowl. Knotted around her neck.

Ori sat on the carved arm of the large wooden armchair, its curlicues poking his bottom. He stared up, at the alien creatures, the damp patches in sinister shapes screeching in silence across the cobwebbed walls, felt them grow before his eyes, a cancerous growth spreading across the walls. Time throbbed, spun around, shot out everywhere.

She lay there, as if strangled by her own hair.

><><

Abir appeared at the door. "What are you doing over here?" Ori wouldn't look at Abir while he called out. "Come on. They want to talk to you."

Ori stood up, tying the sheets of *Dusk* with a rubber band snatched from the dust-coated table. He knew what to do with the story. It had to rise out of its crumbling crevice under the pillow, go and meet the world, flash a pallid and brittle smile.

He walked back through the door into the slippery gleam of Roy's dead-fish eyes staring at him, sleepy but touched with a faint gleam. Dushtu and Nishith rocked in the cradle of fear and glee, lusting for the night when gunpowder would crackle in the air and its pungent odour seep through the darkness. The night of Diwali. When accidents went off like firecrackers from lit cigarettes and then got lost forever in the constellation of lights and flares dotting the evening sky. It was also time they went for a walk downstairs. Stumble across the oddball nooks and hidden exits, the secret wire meshes and the flammable stacks of broken furniture from old sets. This was a theatre like no other, this circular freak show.

"Ori." Abir nodded, a smile swimming in his eyes. "Take Ori along. He's known this place forever."

Perfect. Nishith barely knew this house. God forbid! Neither did Roy, he was no lover of the theatre. Nishith just knew the one thing that mattered. The electric meter, where you could cut off the load to hook up the positive and negative cables to start the show.

If Ori could show him around a little, he would easily find what he had to know. Could Ori do that?

Yes, Ori could.

Wading through the wreckage of an ancient set, Ori breathed in the sharp smell of matches, quickly drowned by the coarse fragrance of cigarette smoke.

29

He picked a time when he knew his mother would not be home. Unhurried, he passed a little shop near the train station, a slice of life stacked with ice cream and Coca-Cola and Limca and other fizzy drinks, writing paper and pens and instant noodles in shiny yellow packets. He tried not to look at the wobbly wooden benches outside the shop that brought up the greasy taste of stale chicken patties on his tongue. A sliver of light flashed before his eyes—the thin glint of a silver watch across a bony, copper-coloured wrist.

He felt the cool of twilight in the heat of the afternoon. He walked faster.

He arrived at a house painted a garish lime-green. He turned the key, opened the lock, and put the key back into his pocket. He still hated the grating noise of the key inside, the way it croaked the lock open. Still hated having to push the door open, to struggle with the rustic resistance of the wood, still unused to being pushed back and forth. The smell of dust and paint from which there was no freedom.

Did he like this place? A place that felt raw, a house that could never be rid of the smell of new paint?

Braving the odour, he walked into the passage.

He stepped into the room, stared at the large table near the window. Everything looked small, little toys playing a game of make-believe. A glass cookie jar with a blue top. A faux-leather case for glasses, softly round, egglike. A little blue jar of Nivea body lotion, a large teacup stacked with lifeless pens, loose sheets of paper with stage directions boldly etched on them. Right in the middle of the table, an unplugged electric iron turned upside down on a bedspread folded together hurriedly.

A crumpled green-and-gold tie hanging from a hook behind the door.

All grown smaller, ready to crumble into powder on the lightest touch. Did life left behind always shrink in size?

Gently, he lifted the iron, cold to his touch, placed the brittle sheets under it. Letters welded to one another in a riverine rhythm. *Dusk*. Brittle, ashen sheets lovingly wrapped in last week's old newspaper. The poor man's brown paper.

It was a place where she couldn't miss it. The tale of Mrinmoy's love for Meera, risen out of its crumbling crevice under an ancient pillow, to meet her, flash a pallid and brittle smile.

Show crooked white teeth. A dead woman noosed with her own braid of hair.

He lay down the key across the litter of pockmarked letters. His key. Never to be lost. Not in school, not in the train, not on the streets. Never.

He stood outside the kitchen, enmeshed in a mild coalescence of terror and sadness. Imagining the northwest corner of the room, where the fat gray lizard clasped the thin yellow one. Imagining them shrunken, withered, dead. Desiccated lizard skeletons swimming in the dust.

His legs felt heavy. He paused at the threshold.

On the table, the rolled-up sheets had unfurled like a slowly blooming flower. In half bloom, it revealed the wrinkled newspaper shrouding the manuscript. It was a newspaper with its heart blackened by a picture of destruction. The ruins of an ancient civilization.

> October 29. *The Pantheon burnt to cinders in catastrophic late-night fire.*

Keyless, he pulled the door gently behind him as he stepped out on the road. The open lock dangled through the chain.

30

The month turned, bringing the early breath of winter, a cool Sunday morning.

Ori sat in his father's room and carefully clipped his nails. The whites of his nails, whenever they pushed ahead, made him uneasy; he did not feel clean till he had clipped them bare again. They felt tougher in the dry air of winter, a little more stubborn. He grimaced as he pressed the clipper hard, biting off a little too much sometimes, baring the pink flesh of his fingertips.

A shadow darkened the door. Mummum stood at the threshold, a frail heap of oldness. How long had it been since she had lumbered around the house, pausing every few feet, watching everything? Certainly it had been years since she had entered this room, the room that had once been his parents'.

"Do not cut your nails today," she said gently.

"What?" he asked. "Why?"

"Go now." She looked away. "To your mother."

"Ma?" His throat dried up. "What happened?"

"Your Baba," she groped at the words slowly, as if they kept floating away from her. "Your Baba has already gone."

"What happened?" he whispered.

"She fell . . ." The old woman's voice wavered. "She fell . . ."

He stared at his grandmother, the nail clipper held firmly in his hand.

And then he remembered. A Hindu did not cut his nails for two weeks following a death in the family.

Suddenly the world blurred, as if he were looking at it through dull, stirred water.

She looked like a goddess. They had done her up beautifully with flowers. Pallabi, they said, had done all of it. The hair, the flowers, and the joss sticks planted around her. White flowers. Jasmine, tuberoses. Evening bloomers all, cold, moist, and graceful, flowers that seemed to melt into her pale, bloodless skin. More and more flowers crowded around her like quiet mourners.

Whispers hushed as Ori sliced through the scattered crowd that had made the dusty, paint-smelling house full of life and warm breath. But the whispers refused to die.

For she had died a death that would make a playwright proud. Drugged, plunging three floors to the ground, shocking an early morning group of laborers on a neighbouring rooftop. Carelessly she had floated to a death that had stunned life.

But why did she let herself be robbed of life so easily? Why didn't she hold on to it, fight it brutally? Why?

The questions buzzed around like flies looking for a place to settle. Ori felt his skin tighten as they came closer. And then they buzzed away, leaving him empty.

A ragged and confused crowd swirled in and around the lime-green house. People from theatre troupes far and near. The rickshaw puller who brought her home every day from the railway station. Her cousin, a reed-thin woman with whom his mother had grown up in a large noisy home, and her husband, a shy amateur photographer whom Ori had always seen in old, dirty pyjamas. The woman who came to sweep and clean the lime-green house every morning. Loudly she was complaining that last month's pay was due today. Now who would pay her?

Ori's father was far in the back. But Ori found him. Slowly he crept closer to him.

The landlord stood, his burly shoulders stooped, humiliated by the police visit to his house. He was going to put up the railings on his terrace. Soon, he murmured. But how could someone slip from there if she didn't want to? He was a good man, and he did not want any trouble.

The thin cousin burst into a spasm of tears. Her meek photographer husband consoled her, touching her lightly, as if he were afraid of her.

Trinankur came and stood next to Ori and his father. He fished out a crumpled piece of paper. "The death certificate, from the corporation. Wasn't easy," he whispered and looked at Ori's father, unsure. "Will you keep it? Or should I give it to them?" He looked at the crying cousin.

It was death by accident.

But still the questions buzzed, the mucky flies with scaly feet.

❧

Rites waited for no one. Not for answers. And the body would not wait.

But they had to wait at the burning ghat. It took a long time before they gave Ori a little flame burning at the end of a length of bent wood. He held his father's hand with his left hand, and with his right, brought the flame to his mother's lips. Blue, ashen lips.

Lighting her lips with fire. Mukhagni. Something for the son to do.

Quickly, the dom, untouchable men who dealt in the dead, pushed the corpse ahead. It slid toward the sluice gate of the electric pyre. The gate lifted, and they heard the muffled roar of the fire. Sharply the gate descended and clanged shut, curtaining off his mother.

Ori hugged his father. "You're crying," he whispered.

They walked through the forest of flowers. Firmly he gripped his father's wrist. "Come," he whispered. "Just hold on to my hand. *Tight* kore."

"Did you show it to anybody?" Her moist voice had hummed on the phone.

"No," he had said. "The play? No one," he whispered. "Just you, Ma."

"I cannot sleep," she had cried. "Not anymore." She merely had to close her eyes to see the hideous last scene.

The dead whore with the braided hair knotted around her neck.

"Where did you find this play?"

Wandering through The Pantheon with the people from the Party. Shuffling through Ahin's things. He knew as soon as he said it that he had made a mistake, and bit his lips so hard that they had threatened to bleed.

"The Pantheon," her words had faded. "Burnt and dead and gone."

She had a lifetime of memories from The Pantheon. A lifetime, she had whispered. Sheaves and sheaves of laughter and play.

"But . . . but what were you doing in The Pantheon with the Party people?" Her voice had sharpened. "Why were you there?"

He had drawn his breath, held it fast.

For a while, she didn't speak. But he could still hear her breathing.

"Ori?" hoarsely, she had asked. "You brought Rana to that play, didn't you?"

He did not speak.

"Rana has become strange," she said. "He has left school. He doesn't want to let go of his mother. Not even for a moment. If Pallabi has a light fever, he becomes paranoid. You knew it would scare him, didn't you? Why . . . ?'" Her voice was barely a whisper when she asked. "You . . . Did you all plan this together? Oh—I—Ori . . ."

He had remained quiet. Dead quiet.

"Ori?" she whispered. "You know what happened in The Pantheon the night of Diwali. Don't you?

"Tell me," her voice wilted. "Tell me, Ori."

He breathed into the phone. Her words tried to scratch at him again. But they scratched nothing. He merely waited.

He waited till she asked no more.

Acknowledgments

Play House is a reincarnated being. It comes to the United States after two entrancing years in India. For this reincarnated life, a great wave of gratitude is due to Chris Knopf, copublisher of The Permanent Press and supple fabulist of mystery novels. Chris's reading of this book will live and echo in my soul for as long as I live and write. It has made me believe that the story of a little boy's destructive obsession with his mother's life as a theatre actor in the lanes of Calcutta can live anew in the distant shores of America.

I'm thankful to Judy and Marty Shepard, copublishers of The Permanent Press, for supporting this book and bringing about its new life. Marty's sharply contagious excitement has made me see this book in new rays of light.

Much credit for *Play House* goes to Barbara Anderson, the efficient and meticulous copy editor for the new edition. I'm also grateful to Pia Bakshi for reading the galleys with a careful set of eyes.

Thanks to the various periodicals that have published excerpts from this novel: *The Kenyon Review*, *World Literature Today*, *Scroll*, *Firstpost*, and *Kitaab*, and to the *Los Angeles*

Review of Books for publishing a conversation between me and the novelist Joe Haske to mark this US edition.

In its Indian life, this novel is called *The Firebird*, and it has been blessed to get much love and excitement in that country. A shout-out to Poulomi Chatterjee, publisher and editor, for continuing to champion this book, and the rest of the team at Hachette India, especially Shobhita Narayan and Avanija Sundarmurti. I am grateful to the writers, readers, journalists, critics, event-crafters, and festival-makers who have given the book their love: Aditya Mani Jha, Amit Chaudhuri, Amit Shankar Saha, Ayan Chattopadhyay, Ananda Lal, Anjum Hasan, Anjum Katyal, Arunava Sinha, Baisali Chatterjee-Dutt, Chandreyee Ghose Dutta, Chandril Bhattacharya, Derek Attridge, Diksha Dutta, Dipanjan Sinha, Elizabeth Kuruvilla, Geetha Chhabra, G.J.V. Prasad, Hansda Sowvendra Shekhar, Jayita Sengupta, Jhimli Mukherjee-Pandey, Jaya Bhattacharjee-Rose, Joe Haske, Keri Walsh, Mahesh Dattani, Maina Bhagat, Malavika Banerjee, Mike Flannery, Mona Sengupta, Mujibur Rehman, Namita Gokhale, Nilanjana Roy, Ragini Tharoor-Srinivasan, Rajat Chaudhuri, Rosinka Chaudhuri, Rudrangshu Mukherjee, Saikat Chakraborty, Saheli Mitra, Sandip Roy, Sanjoy Roy, Satish Padmanabhan, Sharon Marcus, Shuktara Lal, Siddharth Dhanvant Shanghvi, Sohini Chattopadhyay, Sohini Sengupta, Sufia Khatoon, Sumana Roy, Sushrooto Sarkar, Suvasree Karanjai, Tabish Khair, Tom Lutz, Vivek Atray, and Vivek Shanbhag.

As always, the home team—Subhasree, Inaya, and Neer—who have foresuffered all.